Into The Past II

SHAMIKA HILL

INTO THE PAST II

Shamika Hill

Copyright © Shamika Hill

Published in the United States of America by

Shamika Hill

Authoress.shamikah@gmail.com

PROLOGUE

CIERA

Ahh! I love the feeling of my muscles burning from a good workout. The feel of my rapid heartbeat while I work up a sweat from running on the treadmill in the incline position. Eminem's 'Lose Yourself' blared in my ears from my blue tooth earbuds.

I was lost in the words of the song. The beat of the music made me want to push myself to the limits. I was drenched in sweat. I didn't mind. If I wasn't sweating, I wasn't doing it right.

My black and green sports bra and my black spandex leggings clung tightly to my body. My curly hair was in a messy bun. I was so deep in my zone that I didn't notice someone standing beside me until my earbud was removed.

I jumped, startled to see Brayden. His perfect white teeth showed as he smiled back at me. His dark brown eyes stared into my green ones. His long black locs were pulled back into a ponytail. He wore a white Puma shirt with red basketball shorts and a pair of red and white Pumas.

"Oh, my bad, shorty. I didn't mean to scare you. What I tell you about following me?" He smiled.

"Boy!" I cut my eyes at him, slightly irritated about him taking out my earbud. I hate being interrupted when working out, especially when I'm in the zone. "Ain't nobody following you," I snapped in between breaths while still running on the treadmill. "Did you forget my dad owns this place?"

"How could I? He's my boss. Speaking of your dad, have you told him about us yet?" He asked as he handed my earbud back to me.

I turned the treadmill off and grabbed my towel draped across the machine. "No. Not yet." I said, still out of breath as I wiped the sweat from my forehead and chest. I knew where this conversation was going. I rolled my eyes, coming down from my workout high.

"Damn, CeCe! What are you waiting on?" He said as he turned around to sit on the weight bench across from me. "It's been about three months since we started dating. That man gone beat my ass when he finds out."

"It's complicated," I exhaled, still drying off my face.

"You're the one making this shit complicated. I can't avoid Glen when I come up here. You got me talking to this man knowing I'm dating his daughter, and he doesn't know about it. This is the type of shit that can get a nigga killed. Your dad's old school. I'm going to tell him myself."

"Listen," I stepped off the treadmill. "I don't want to talk about this here. My dad got eyes and ears everywhere."

"Man… I ain't try'in to hear that shit." He said, shaking his head.

"Brayden, you only know Glen as your boss. You can go home after work and not be bothered by him. I, on the other hand, live with that man. I think him being a father is more difficult than being your boss!" I said, trying my best not to be too loud. I was getting so tired of having this conversation with him. I was starting to sound like a broken record.

"I'm giving you forty-eight hours, CeCe. That's forty-eight hours to tell that man, or I will. This is ridiculous. You're making me look bad. Woman up and stop acting like a damn kid." He said while getting up.

"Excuse me! Woman up! You might think you know my father, and you may think he likes you, but once he finds out we are dating, he'll be mopping the floor with your face as an example to every employee up here. I will tell my father when I'm good and ready, not before." I said as I walked past him. "We can always call it quits if you're worried about looking bad. Don't nobody know we're dating anyway." I said, irritated, that he gave me a time frame.

He jumped up, grabbed my wrist, pulled me into him, and kissed my cheek.

"Nope. I'm already committed to this thing. You don't have to look out for me. I can handle your dad. It was he who trained me, after all." He said, holding onto my waist.

"And you a fool if you think he taught you everything he knows."

"Whatever, CeCe. I'm about to go shoot some hoops with the fellas. Are we still on for tonight?"

"Yeah."

"Cool. I'll pick you up at eight."

"Don't pick me up from my house. I'll be at Jessica's. I'll text you the address."

He shook his head as he turned to walk out of the gym. "Forty-eight hours, CeCe!" He yelled before walking out the door.

"I'm not in the mood to be tried!" I yelled back as I grabbed my duffle bag and headed to the showers. I had a lunch date with my co-worker and refused to be late.

****

I was the first to arrive at Sergio's and decided to get a patio table while I waited for Jessica. Sergio's was an Italian restaurant in the middle of an outdoor shopping center.

Although it was a hot summer day, the strong breeze made the sun's warmth tolerable. Despite how hot it was, it was too nice of a day to be cooped up inside a restaurant with a crowd of people trying to keep cool from the heat. Just as I decided to text Jessica to let her know, I got us a table. I look up at the sound of her loud voice.

"Aye, Chica!" She yelled, just as loud as always.

Jessica had an accent. The way she talked always reminded me of Sofia Vergara. Jessica was biracial, Puerto Rican, and Black. Her thick, curly hair was loose, with one side pinned up. Jessica smiled bright, her full red lips accented her copper-colored skin and played off her light freckles. She wore a black spaghetti tank top with dark blue jeans.. Her black thong sandals made a clapping sound with every step that she took.

I met Jessica last month at my interview at Ami's Boutique. We didn't talk much that day but hit it off fast once my training began.

"Aye, lady! Why are you always early when we go out to eat, but you're late to everything else?" She said as I stood up to hug her.

"I'm not always late. You make me sound greedy." I laughed.

"You are greedy. You get away with it because you live at the gym." She said as we took our seats.

"That's where I'm trying to get you to go. You should come with me one day."

"Oh no, Chica. I ain't trying to do nothing to risk losing this ass or my girls." She said, cupping her breasts and squeezing them.

"Why are you so extra? Just tone up." I laughed.

"Nope, I got my way of toning. I don't need no gym."

"Hi, ladies. My name is Mark. I will be your waiter today. Are you ready to order?"

"Aye, Papi! How can we order with no menus?'" Jessica said while crossing her arms across her chest.

"I'm sorry… here you go." The waiter pulls out two menus from his apron pocket. "Did you want anything to drink while you read over the menu?"

"Yes. Can I have a coke zero, please?" I answered.

"Coke zero!" Jessica yells. "See, that's what I'm talking about, Chica. A little sugar won't kill you. Live a little."

"Have you ever tasted Coke zero? It's sweet."

"Oy, but it has no sugar." Jessica turns back to the waiter. "I'll take a sprite, please."

"Sure thing. I'll be back shortly to take your order." He says before turning to walk away.

"Don't hurry back. I don't like to be rushed." Jessica says loud enough for the waiter to hear her.

"Yes, ma'am." He says before continuing to walk on.

"Why do you have to be so rude, Jessi?"

"I'm not being rude. I just don't like to be rushed."

"Rushed! Girl, you didn't even need to ask for a menu. As much as we come here, we already know the menu by heart."

"Yeah, but he doesn't know that. He looks new." She laughed. "So, how's Brielle doing? I heard she was in an accident."

"Yeah, she's alright. I haven't seen her yet, but I heard she has second-degree burns on her arm and hand."

"Ouch! What happened?"

"It's a long story."

"Ooh… it sounds like you got some tea! So, spill it, Chica."

I look at her in disbelief. I can't believe she thinks I'm about to sit here and gossip about my cousin. "No, Jessica! You stay trying to get into other people's business. You're so nosy."

"Here you go, ladies." The waiter said as he approached our table, handing us our drinks. "Here's your coke zero, and here is your Sprite."

"Thanks," I said before he walked off.

"I'm not nosy. I'm just concerned. Brielle's my friend, too." I shrugged my shoulders, not caring that she has known Brielle for over a year. Brielle is the manager for Ami's Boutique, it was because of her that I was hired. Despite Jessica's claim at them being friends, I only know them as coworkers. Not once have I seen the two of them hang out outside of work.

"Well, it's not my story to tell."

"You're no fun." She said with a frown as she took a sip of her drink.

"I just don't like drama."

"Oh! We should have a girls' night at her house. That would be fun."

I just shook my head. There was no winning with her. This was just another attempt at her trying to get into my cousin's business. I enjoyed hanging out with Jessica. Besides her love for gossip, she seems like a good person. Plus, I loved her spiciness.

"I'll see if and when I can set something up," I groaned, giving in. "My dad asked me to give Brielle and her mom some space. So, it probably won't be anytime soon."

"Oh, it must be serious if they asked you to give her some space. You guys are so close."

"I know. We're like sisters, so you can understand how I can be overprotective of her with you trying to be in her business," I said with seriousness before taking a sip of my drink.

Jessica takes another sip of her drink and then rolls her eyes. "I wish I had a sister because my half gets on my damn nerves. Oy, here he comes now." She rolled her eyes.

"Your what?" I laughed. "Would you stop calling him your half? Girl, that's your brother."

"Yeah, I know. My half-brother." She said with a look of disgust on her face. She always acts like she can't stand him, yet she's overprotective of her big brother. They have the same father but different mothers.

"Why are you always popping up on me? Don't you have a life?" Jessica yelled out as he approached our table.

Keon walked towards us with a smile on his face. He didn't resemble Jessica at all except for the eyes. Keon wasn't biracial like Jessica. Both of his parents were black.

Keon was three years older than Jessica. From what I hear, they've always been close, even when Jessica lived in Puerto Rico with her mom. She moved to the U.S. to live with her dad six months ago.

Keon was a little darker than Jessica, with his almond-colored skin tone. He wore his hair in a low-cut fade and had a dimple on his left cheek. He looked clean in his white sneakers, black joggers and a white shirt that read King in black writing. Seeing Jessica and Keon together, you would have never known they were siblings. They have different personalities much like their difference in looks.

Keon bent down to give Jessica a forehead Kiss. Then, he turned his attention to me. "What's up, CeCe? You look beautiful as always." I smiled at his compliment, but Jessica cut in before I could respond.

"Hello, Keon!" Jessica waived her hand in his face. "You started flirting with my friend before you answered my question. I bump into you more now than before you moved out of Daddy's house. What are you doing here?" She said, rolling her eyes.

"I ordered food to-go. I only came by to pick it up. Calm down, Jessi."

The waiter returned to our table. I couldn't help but notice his nervousness. "Are you ready to order?" He asked me, trying to avoid eye contact with Jessica.

"Yes. I'll have the baked rigatoni and a Caesar salad." I said, handing him back the menu. I didn't even glance at it. I knew this place like the back of my hand.

"Ok." He responded as he wrote in his notepad and grabbed the menu from me. I could see him visibly relax upon taking my order. "For you, Miss?" He asked, looking at Jessica.

"Let me have the pasta primavera. Can you add chicken and shrimp with that?"

"No problem. Will you be dining, as well, sir?" He asked Keon.

"Naw, I'm good."

"Okay. I'll be back with your order." He says just before walking off.

"What did you order, Keon, pizza?" Jessica asked, looking up at her brother.

"Yep. You already know." He replied.

Jessica shook her head. "How do you come to an Italian restaurant and only get pizza?"

"How can you come here and not get pizza?" He asked.

"Whatever. Can you keep my seat warm? I have to run to the lady's room."

"Sure." He smiled, sitting down in Jessica's chair the moment she got up.

"Don't be harassing my friend while I'm gone, either." She warned, giving him a side eye as she walked away. He just shooed her on.

"So, what's up, CeCe? You still talking to Bryan?"

"You mean Brayden." I corrected him with a smirk.

I first met Keon about a month after I started dating Brayden. Ironically, I didn't know he was Jessica's brother until yesterday. Imagine my surprise when I spotted him dropping Jessica off at Ami's boutique. Keon has always shown interest in me, and I gotta admit the man is sexy as hell but I made it a point not to lead him on. I'm not the type to step out on my man and I'm very much committed to Brayden even though I haven't yet outed our relationship to my folks. Brayden and I dine at Sergio's often and Brayden has run into us here a few times. Keon knows very well who Brayden is. So, I don't take his harmless flirting seriously.

"Whatever! He picked up my drink and took a sip.

"Really! Excuse you!" I snapped while taking my glass from him. "I don't know you like that." He quickly grabbed my hand after I sat the glass down, holding it tightly so I couldn't snatch it away.

"Well, let's change that." He says as he starts massaging my hand.

I'd be lying if I said he wasn't putting me in a trance, but this little hand massage was on point. My eyes relaxed on his as he kneaded the palm of my hand down to my fingers. The warmth of his hands made my body melt a little more than it should.

"I can't. You know I'm in a relationship with… um… Br-Brayden." I stuttered, speaking slowly.

"Now that's a problem… but not one that can be easily solved."

"What are you talking about, Keon?" I asked, his hands still working down my fingers.

"I can't make you the future, Mrs. Wright, if you think you still have a future with that clown." He kissed my hand before letting go. "I don't like that guy. Can I borrow your phone? I need to make a call. Before you even ask, I left my phone in the car."

"How can you not like someone when you don't even know him?" I asked as I unlocked my phone and handed it to him.

He took the phone and immediately started dialing a number. "I don't need to know him. He's trying to claim someone that doesn't belong to him. Here." He says, giving me back my phone. "I put my number in your phone."

"You got some nerve. What makes you think I want your number?" I said as I checked my phone.

"The look on your face when I massaged your hand."

I shook my head in disbelief. That was the oldest trick in the book, and I fell for it.

"You know Jessica is my friend, right? How would she feel if she found out you were making passes at me?"

"Are you kidding! Once we're married, she'll finally have the sister she always wanted. All she ever talks about is how much she wants a sister. She'll probably go off on you for standing in the way of that." He laughed, shrugging his shoulders. "I have to get out of here. Tell Jessica I said I'll catch her later." He said as he got up to leave.

I shook my head. "You're too arrogant. That's not a good look."

"Only when it comes to my future. If you feel like I'm coming on too strong. I'll fall back some." He says as he bends down and kisses my forehead. "Oh, before I forget, I got your number too." He whispers in my ear, smiling at me before he walks out of the patio area towards the lobby.

"Where did my half go?" Jessicca questioned walking up to our table.

"He left. Your brother is sneaky. He stole my phone number." I said as I leaned back in my chair. He's going to get me in trouble."

"That bastard! How long ago did he leave?" She asked, pretending to be upset. Her smile lets me know she's happy with the games her brother is playing. For all I know, this whole situation was set up.

I looked past her, just as someone caught my eye. "He… he ah… he left a couple of minutes ago," I answered, still staring past her. "Is that… I think that's Brayden."

Jessica turned around to see who I was looking at. "If that is, he looks mad."

"I just saw him before I came here. He wasn't wearing that." Just as quickly as I spotted him, he was gone. If it was Brayden, I would have some explaining to do. Depending on how long he was watching me.

After an afternoon of shopping and goofing around, we finally made it back to Jessica's house. We watched movies and ate popcorn until I noticed the time. It was just after 8:30, and Brayden was late. I checked my phone to see if I had any missed calls. Nope, I thought to myself after checking my phone.

Jessica was still very much into the movie when I decided to call Brayden. I waited for him to answer. It wasn't like him to be late.

"What time is Brayden supposed to be here?" She questioned noticing I was on my phone.

"Eight."

"Looks like you got stood up, Chica. Nothing worse than being dressed for a date and then being stood up with nowhere to go."

"He's never late," I answered, a little worried.

"Did you try calling?"

"Yeah. No answer."

"Well, try to relax. There's nothing more you can do right now. I'm sure Brayden's okay. You want some more popcorn?"

Deciding to take her up on her offer, I grabbed the popcorn bowl from her. She was right. Bayden didn't answer the phone, and I didn't know where he was. For all I knew, he could be upset about what he saw at Sergio's. So, I decided to enjoy the movie.

It was ten-thirty by the time the movie was over. I figured it was time to go home since I had nowhere else to go. Not to mention, Jessica had work in the morning. Standing up I started gathering my things, I didn't want to be the cause of her tiredness, I wouldn't hear the end of it. My phone rang, startling me. I quickly answered it, thinking it was Brayden.

I answered without looking at the caller ID ready to give Brayden a piece of my mind. "You got some...."

"Ciera! Where are you?" My dad asked frantically, cutting me off. I knew this wouldn't be a good phone call by the urgency of his voice. He sounded on edge, on the verge of cussing someone out and crying his heart out. My heart started beating faster as I waited for the reason for his call.

"I'm at Jessica's house. Is everything okay?"

"There's been a break-in at Brenda's. She and Brielle are hurt. Meet us at Hope Memorial."

"Oh, my God! Are they okay?" I asked frantically.

"Just get there now!" He yelled before hanging up.

"What's going on? What happened?" Jessica asked, grabbing my arm. I stood there momentarily in shock from the information I had just received. "Ciera!" Jessica yelled, knocking me out of my trance. Suddenly, my head was pounding. I started seeing spots and fell onto the couch, hoping my dizziness would subside quickly.

"Um... I ... I have to go." I said, getting up and gathering my things. I moved slowly as I tried to process what my father said. Part of my brain was telling me to hurry up, yet I felt numb and confused wondering if I heard him correctly."

"Cece! What's going on? Is everything okay?"

"My aunt Brenda and Brielle were hurt in a break-in. They're being rushed to the hospital as we speak." It seemed like saying it out loud snapped me back into reality. I quickly looked in my bags, making sure I grabbed everything. "I need to get to the hospital."

Jessica gasped as she covered her mouth. "Oh, my God! I'm coming with you? You shouldn't be alone right now." She grabbed her purse, keys, and phone from the coffee table.

"No... I'll be fine. I just have to get there. I'll call you and keep you posted." I assured her with a shaky voice as I rushed out the door. I was on autopilot. My arms felt heavy and my legs wobbly as I headed toward the door. I kept trying to remind myself to breathe as I concentrated on my steps. Trying to will my legs not to fall from under me.

"Okay. Call me if you need me." Jessica said as she followed me to the door.

I slowed down when I noticed a couple parked behind my car. I know Brayden has a silver Infiniti Q60 coupe, but I couldn't tell what color or model the car was in the darkness. It was what the driver was doing that had me in shock. I watched him as he punched himself in the head before he screamed out and repeatedly punched the steering wheel.

"Who is that?" Jessica asked slowly as she turned her porch light on. The driver looked at us, turned the car on, and quickly sped away from the house.

"I don't know. It looks like Brayden's car, but I couldn't tell what color it was." I replied before rushing again to meet my family at the hospital.

CHAPTER 1

Ciera

One year later

Three... two... one... Happy New Year! We all screamed together after watching the ball drop on the seventy-five-inch tv hanging on the wall. Some of us toasted the new year with a champagne flute; others enjoyed their first kiss of the year, hoping it would bring them luck in the love department. This year, we hosted our annual New Year's party at the Grand Mar Hotel in the penthouse.

This place is beautiful. There are two levels of wall to wall floor to ceiling curtained windows and a beautiful circular staircase off the side of the room. The white and gold tile flooring made the black and gold decorations stand out more.

The penthouse was adorned with beautiful black and white furniture throughout the first and second floors, giving ample space for guests to lounge and relax. The center of the room was designated for dancing. Servers walked around the penthouse dressed in elegant attire. Black slacks, long white sleeve shirts, black vests, and a black bow tie, which complimented the color scheme. They sauntered around with trays of champagne and hors d'oeuvres, carefully passing them out to the guests.

I look around at everyone wearing their all-black, dressed to kill. Everyone partnered up with smiles on their faces with hopes of new beginnings. I couldn't help but feel alone. Brielle was off somewhere with Loyal, and I was dateless. I was happy until the moment everyone screamed 'happy new year'.' I'm unsure if it was because I was lonely or worried about what was coming. I get like this every new year. I guess you can say it's fear of the unknown. Whichever one it was, it gave me chills. I'm so grateful my family and I made it to see another year, and I hope and pray that this year is as good or at least, better than the last.

I look out onto the dance floor and notice my mom and dad grinding on each other dancing to Poison by Bell Biv DeVoe. My dad dipping it low, with a glass of champagne in his hand.

I spotted Aunt Brenda and Uncle Gerald on the dance floor, working up a sweat of their own. I scanned the room again, looking for Brielle and Loyal. I still can't find them, but I know they're together. These days, you can't find one without the other. They have been inseparable ever since Brielle came home from the hospital.

I suddenly felt like the walls were closing in on me. I stand up while drinking the rest of my champagne and quickly place the flute on the server's tray as he passes.

As I head outside to get some air, I gaze at my reflection in the window as I walk towards the door. My long black sequin cameo dress with a thigh-high split on my right leg and six-inch black wrap-around stilettos. My hair was in a low bun updo with a flat twist, and my edges laid as always. My gold dangle earrings and bracelets sparkled in my reflection. I was happy with what I saw.

I reached the rooftop garden and went straight to the railing, taking in a deep breath while looking out at the city. I'm always mesmerized by all the city lights and passing cars, wondering where everyone is going.

"Happy new year!" Brielle said, startling me. I turned around, seeing her and Loyal snuggled up on the black and gray outdoor sectional, in front of the fire pit table.

"Hey, I was wondering where you two ran off to. Happy new year." I said as I took a seat on the sectional across from them.

"You look like you got a lot on your mind," Loyal said.

"I don't know... maybe. I feel kind of weird, lonely... maybe both. It's hard to describe." I sighed, leaning in towards the fire pit while rubbing my hands together to absorb the heat.

"Are you here alone?" Loyal asked.

"Yeah."

"What! Why? I thought you were going to invite Keon." Brielle asked.

"I was, but I changed my mind at the last minute. I thought it would be awkward if Brayden showed up while I was here with Keon. I don't want any drama."

"Why do you even care what Brayden thinks? He had his chance. Now you over here depressed and alone." Brielle said.

She was right. It's been a year with no word from Brayden. I don't know why I still cared about his feelings. He made it very clear that he didn't care about mine.

"Why did you two stop talking anyway?" Loyal asked.

"I'm not sure, honestly. Brayden may have seen Keon flirting with me when I went out with Jessica a while back. He was supposed to pick me up that night but stood me up."

"Damn! He doesn't speak when you see him at the office? I know you've ran into him since then?" Brielle asked.

"I did. He just ignored me, stopped answering my calls and everything. I was stood up, with no call or explanation as to what happened." I answered, staring into the flames while enjoying the warmth it gave.

"Well, I don't think you should worry about that guy. A real man would say what he has to say instead of ghosting his lady. Not to mention, that guy seems a little off to me. I don't trust him." Loyal said, sounding irritated.

Brielle sat up and turned around to get a better look at him. "You've met Brayden?"

"Yeah. A couple of weeks ago. I went to the office to chat with your dad and Glen." He answered.

Brielle's face frowned as if she was either confused or upset. "About what?" She asked.

Loyal turned her around so that her back was against him. "Men stuff. Why you gotta be in my business, woman?" He laughed. "Am I not allowed to conversate with Glen or Gerald?"

"I didn't know you; my dad and Uncle Glen were so close." She said.

"Anyway, CeCe, it's good that your dad didn't know about him. What was Brayden like thirty-seven, thirty-eight years old? Your pops wouldn't have liked the age gap." Loyal said.

"Dang! You know his age, too!" Brielle said, looking back at Loyal. He laughed, hugging her tightly.

"He was thirty-nine, actually," I admitted.

"Thirty-nine CeCe? You were twenty-one when you started talking to him." Brielle said, bringing her attention back to me. "Is that why you didn't want to tell your dad about him?"

"Part of it… but in my defense, Brayden didn't act or look his age."

"Shiiit, that nigga looked like he was in his late thirties. You were just feeling his old ass. That's why you couldn't see it." Loyal laughed.

"Well, it's good that Uncle Glen didn't know…."

"Didn't know what?" My dad asked as he, my mom, Uncle Gerald, and Aunt Brenda made their way over to us with drinks and smiles. Aunt Brenda and Uncle Gerald were still dancing as they made their way over to us.

"Don't know that I'm not your Goddaughter," Brielle said, keeping our conversation between us. I wasn't surprised. Brie was never the type to spill tea. She hated gossip.

"Shit… I wish Gerald would take my title away. He gone get a taste of these size twelve." He taunted, taking a seat next to CeCe.

Uncle Gerald laughed. "Yo, my man… is that a threat?" He asked, twirling his champagne around in his flute with a big grin. Uncle Gerald lived for a challenge.

"It seems like you forgot about the knuckle sandwiches I used to feed you back in the day. You hungry, brah?" He laughed.

"Would you two stop!" Aunt Brenda chuckled, pushing Gerald down beside Loyal and Brielle and sitting on his lap. "You two always act like kids when you're together. It's a wonder how y'all even got a business started. You two can't go a day without challenging each other."

"Well, he started it!" Uncle Glen said, pointing to Uncle Gerald.

"And I plan on finishing it. Just wait till we get to work on Monday, baby boy." Uncle Gerald said as Aunt Brenda took a sip from his flute.

"So y'all got any plans for the new year?" Aunt Brenda asked, looking at me, Brielle, and Loyal."

"Nope. Just finishing my masters." Brielle answered.

"What about you, Ciera? My mom asked, already knowing my plans.

I felt my mom always worried about me returning to my old ways. Not working, taking one class a week, and forcing them to care for me. Over the last year, I have grown a lot. I still work at Ami's part-time and go to school full-time. My life has become busy between work, school, and friends, and I still find time to hit the gym. What I love the most is that my relationship with my mom has improved significantly. There are no arguments between us anymore. I actually enjoy hanging out with her.

"Same as Brie, except I'm working on my bachelor's," I answered.

"Hey, where is Keon? I thought you said he was going to meet us here." My dad asked, looking around.

"Oh, I changed my mind. I didn't invite him."

"You see that, Sherry?" My dad pouted, pulling my mom onto his lap. "She finally brings home a guy I like and doesn't even invite him to our party. I'm so disappointed in you, Ciera."

My mom hits him on the shoulder, laughing. "Glen! Maybe she would have if you would stop stealing him from her whenever he comes around."

"What do you expect, woman! I live in a house with nothing but women. I'm outnumbered. So yeah, I get a little excited when another man comes over."

"Touché." Uncle Gerald says, laughing as he holds up his flute, followed by my dad. They both toast the air.

My mom was right. Don't get me wrong, I'm glad my dad likes Keon. However, it's irritating how he's constantly bugging me about inviting him somewhere. When Keon does come around, I barely get to spend time with him. He's always pulling him away to talk about so-called "men's stuff." I glanced at the party crowd through the window.

"Dad, it looks like your crowd is thinning out."

"Yea, they tend to do that after the countdown. Afterward, everyone runs off to be with their family. They've been here all night. Hell, I'm even ready to go. What about y'all?" He asked.

"I've been ready," I answered honestly. I felt like the seventh wheel. Everyone coupled up, and I'm over here, worried about Brayden's feelings, spending New Year's alone. The hell with Brayden.

"I'm actually ready, too. I have a big day tomorrow." Loyal yawned while sitting up and stretching.

"What do you have going on tomorrow?" Brielle asked.

"I'm throwing a New Year's barbecue tomorrow." He answered.

My mom and dad had odd looks as they exchanged glances. Uncle Glen and Aunt Brenda were smiling and whispering something to my parents.

"Oh, I didn't know you had plans," Brielle shrugged her shoulders.

"What you mean you didn't know. You are going to be there, right?" Loyal asked.

"I wasn't invited," Brielle replied.

"What do you mean you weren't invited.? When have you ever known me to go anywhere without you on my arm?" Loyal asked, looking insulted. Then, he turned his gaze to our parents. "You guys didn't tell her about the barbeque?"

"I thought she knew." They all said in unison.

I couldn't keep a straight face if my life depended on it. They all looked so guilty. The awkward smiles on their faces were like the icing on the cake for me. I shook my head, wanting so badly to call them out. But, instead, Brielle looks over at me.

"Don't look at me. I wasn't told about a barbeque. I'm just laughing at them," I said, pointing to our parents.

"Well, you might be going without me, bae. I'm so tired from all this dancing. I just want to stay in and mellow out tomorrow." Brielle said, standing up.

"Well, good, because the barbeque is at your house," Loyal smiled as if he won the battle.

"Wait, what?" Brielle responded with a look of defeat on her face.

That was it for me. I was laughing so hard my abs were burning. The look of hurt, betrayal, and defeat all rolled into one. This was a perfect start to my new year.

"We about to head out. I'll catch y'all later, Glen." Uncle Gerald announced while slapping my dad's hand. "Happy new year again. Y'all be safe." he smiled, as he embraced my mom. Aunt Brenda followed his lead, passing out hugs.

"Right back at cha." My dad replied, getting up from his seat.

"Brielle, are you riding with us?" Her mom asked her.

"I can drop her off." Loyal offered.

"Alright, we'll see you at the house. Be safe." Uncle Gerald said to Brielle before turning to walk out with Aunt Brenda.

My parents followed close behind and I stood up to join them. "That's my ride, so I'll see y'all at the barbeque tomorrow. Ciao." I blew a kiss to both Loyal and Brielle and walked away smiling.

CHAPTER 2

Brayden

"Happy fuckin new year to me." I say out loud as I take a sip of my Budweiser.

It took me one year. One year to save up enough money to get my new place. Working extra hours at Diamond Watch Securities was the hardest thing I ever had to do. It took everything in me to smile at the Taylors when I really wanted to rip the soul out of each of them and feed it to the devil himself. I hated everything about Glen and Gerald. From the sound of their voices straight down to the cocky ass way they walk. As if they were untouchable. I wanted so badly to blow a hole in their chests. Do the same thing to them that they did to my brother. I had to keep reminding myself that their time would come. I had to be patient a little longer to organize my plans.

The original plan was solid. Mason and I wanted to work for them and become their best employees. Work our way from the bottom to the top hoping they will see us as the sons they never had, maybe even leave us the company one day. But, even if they didn't, we would still come out good. Diamond Watch Securities took care of their employees financially, mentally, and physically. Unfortunately, plans changed when Mason didn't get hired. So, instead of trying to acquire the company legally, we decided to scam our way in.

Mason chose to go after Gerald, he had a personal vendetta against the nigga since he was the one who denied his employment. His plan was to take out Gerald and marry Brenda.

He started casing the house, following them, learning their routines. I knew that both brothers ran the company equally, so if Gerald was on borrowed time, so was Glen. I had Sherry as my target way into the company, but Ciera let it slip that if something happened to her dad, the company would be left to her. Therefore, I decided CeCe would be my way in. I didn't mind wifing her up, she was easy on the eyes, and her body screamed to be snatched.

She was a little young for my taste. Still, I figured I could easily shape her into the type of woman I needed. After befriending the family from the inside and spending extra time with CeCe, it became clear that these women had their own dreams and ambitions. Ain't no way they would want to run a multimillion-dollar company.

I don't know what happened on the day of my brother's death. Everything was going smoothly until I caught Keon flirting with Ciera at Sergio's. I had watched their whole exchange. I didn't have romantic feelings for Ciera, at least not yet. I had too much going on trying to plan how to get away with two murders.

However, I couldn't help but feel some way about their exchange. Keon would have to get dealt with and fast, and Ciera would learn that her actions have consequences and repercussions. As far as I was concerned, she was mine whether she wanted to be or not. I left without causing a scene. I had to meet with Mason to review last-minute details and hand over some equipment. He felt that it was time to put our plan into action.

I arrived at Jessica's house around seven-thirty and parked in front of 'her house behind CeCe's car and called my brother, not knowing that would be my last time hearing his voice.

"Hey, Mason."

"What's up, big bro!" He answered.

"Where you at?" I asked.

"My future house."

"Why are you there so early?"

"Just watch'in. Not much movement today."

"Are they home?"

"Yep, all three of them. I pulled up just in time to see Brielle close the garage door. Gerald's car is in the garage. Brenda's is in the driveway.

"Mason, I think we should do this another day. I got a bad feeling about this man. I thought we agreed to act when he was home alone. We don't need Brielle or her mom getting hurt. If they see you, it could ruin everything." Something didn't sit right with me. I knew that Mason had the tendency to move without thinking. At times, he thought he was invincible.

"Man... I ain't try'in to hear that shit! I'm tired of watching this nigga walk around here like he got the damn world in his hand. He about due for a wakeup call."

"I feel like I should be there with you."

"Naw man... you good. I thought you had something planned with Ciera."

"I do," I said, reclining back in the driver's seat of my car, trying to suppress the weird feeling that had my stomach in knots. "I caught that nigga Keon pushing up on her today," I said while staring at Jessica's house.

"You better handle that. Lil nigga gone fuck around and weasel his way in. Don't let him take what's yours. You need to teach that bitch CeCe a lesson about mingling with the opposite sex." He laughed with seriousness in his voice.

"I plan on it. So, let's get you set up. I'm supposed to pick up CeCe at eight. It's almost eight now." I said as I took out my laptop. "I'm going to pair your camera with my laptop so I can see what the hell is going on since you don't want me to come by.

"Naw, big bro. You can be with me from a distance."

"That's the plan. You got the earpiece with you, too?"

"Yeah."

"Good, let's see if we can get that hooked up also." It took over an hour and a half to get everything hooked up. I also had to troubleshoot the earpiece so he could hear me. "Listen, Mase… make sure you put that camera near the buttons on your shirt."

"I ain't wearing no button shirt."

"Damn, well put it on your collar."

"How's that? We good?"

"Yeah, I can see perfectly. Now, try the earpiece. Hang up, though, so we don't get no interference." I told him.

"Aight." He says just before the line disconnects. I look at the computer, watching him fiddle with the earpiece before putting it in his ear.

"Can you hear me?" I asked through my microphone.

"Yeah, am I good?"

"Yeah. Well, we're all set. What time do you plan on hitting this house?"

"Right now." He said as he started pulling his keys from the ignition and gathering his things.

"What do you mean right now? You see what time it is? It's too early. They might not be sleeping. If you are going to do this while Brielle and Brenda are home, at least wait until they're asleep!" I yelled in frustration. "You are about to mess this whole thing up. If you get caught, ain't no coming back from that."

"Yo stop tripp'in. If I get caught, we'll just come up with another plan. It's now or never, so shut up and watch." He said as he closed the car door.

"Aye, man, don't tell me to shut up! What the fuck we come up with a plan for if you not gone follow it? I'm supposed to be with CeCe right now. You mess 'in everything up. Man, get your ass back in the car!" I yelled.

He continued to walk towards the house, searching for the house key on the key ring.

"If you don't stop screaming in my damn ear, I'm gone beat your ass when I see you. Now keep your eyes open."

All I could do was shake my head and take a deep breath. It didn't seem I had any say in the matter. It's been like this since we were little. Mason always acted impulsively, and I was patient and planned things out. The fact that he couldn't feel pain made him careless. Had him thinking he was fuckin Superman or some shit.

I held my breath when he entered the house, and the light came on. Brenda and Brielle would be sitting on the damn couch, looking at the door.

"Really! I told your ass you were too early"!" I shouted.

I was in shock thinking about how our whole plan had just blown up right before my eyes. I'm sure Mason didn't put on his face mask. I was so busy trying to get him back in the car that I forgot to remind him. I could hear Brenda and Mason exchanging words in the background. I was so caught up in formulating a new play that I didn't know Brielle was missing. I opened my mouth to ask where Brielle went, but I heard a loud thud before any words could come out, and then the camera fell to the floor.

"Mason! You, okay?" I knew he was on the ground. I didn't hear his voice or movement coming from him. Plus, I heard Brielle ask if she had killed him. "Get up!!" My heart felt like it would beat right out of my damn chest. I sat my seat back up. "Mason, can you hear me? Get up, bro!" I yelled.

I could hear talking between Brenda and Brielle, but Mason wasn't answering me. There was a sudden movement from the camera. I saw Brenda fall to the floor. The camera must have still been attached to Mason's collar. I witnessed the moment Mason got up, followed by Brielle coming at my brother with blows to his gut. I'm sure he wasn't hurt since he couldn't feel pain, but the blows to his abdomen were causing him to lose his balance. The next thing I knew, the camera's view dropped, and Brielle's face was level with the camera.

I'm guessing Mason fell to his knees. I could see Brielle throwing punches. "Come on, Bro! One good hit is all you need. Knock her ass out!" I yelled in his ear.

I watched as he threw a solid punch to her face. Her head flew back, causing her to lose her balance, but she came back fast. I saw her spin around, and then a knee came up toward my brother's face. The next thing I knew, my brother was down again.

I yelled in anger, "Shit! Dammit, Mason!"

I assumed Brielle had fighting skills, shit her dad knew like four different fighting styles that I knew of. I figured he would have taught her. That's why the plan was for her and her mother to not be home or at least be asleep.

I couldn't take it anymore. I closed my laptop, threw it in the passenger seat, leaned back on the headrest, and closed my eyes. I didn't know what to do. I thought about going over to him, but it made no sense for both of us to go to jail.

"Ugh! Why couldn't you just listen to me for once!" I screamed out. "Shit!" I yelled as I punched the steering wheel.

It was hard to think of what to do next while the sound of fighting and furniture being tossed was still coming from the laptop. I just stared at the night sky while listening to all the commotion when it suddenly went quiet. I heard Brielle ask her mom if he was dead. I quickly grabbed my laptop and opened it up. All I could see was the ceiling.

"Mason... Mason... Can you hear me? There was no answer. All I could hear was Brielle talking to her mother. "Mason, man, get up!" I held my breath, willing him to speak to me, even if it was just a whisper. "Mason, get up, bro. You gotta get out of there, man. You're getting your ass kicked. Get up!" I yelled.

The next thing I knew, Brenda was on the floor, and Brielle was flying across the room. I felt nothing but relief knowing that my brother was still alive.

"What are you doing, man... get out of there!" I screamed as he walked over to Brielle. He straddles her, then starts choking her and banging her head against the floor. "Mason! What the hell are you doing? Don't kill her! Leave her alone, man. You gotta get out of there!" I screamed, unsure if he could hear me.

The whole time I had been screaming into the microphone, he hadn't acknowledged me not once. It was as if I was watching a horror film. Brielle's eyes started rolling back, at that exact moment, I heard the front door open.

"What the hell! Get the fuck off, my daughter!"

The camera turns toward the figure rushing for Mason. I knew it was Gerald. He struck Mason so hard that the camera flew off him, and I caught a glimpse of Mason flying backward. I heard a loud crack sound, and Mason's bloody face was lying down facing the camera. His eyes were still open. It took a moment before my brain registered what I saw on my screen, my brother was dead. I closed my laptop and threw it. I took my anger out on not only myself but my car, too. It wasn't until I noticed Ciera and Jessica staring at me that I took off. At that moment, I decided to pay them back for what they did to my brother. I wanted Glen and Gerald to know what this pain felt like.

CHAPTER 3

Brielle

"Brie… wake up beautiful," Loyal said while gently rocking my leg back and forth. It's almost as if he were singing his words as he spoke, trying to wake me up.

I slowly open my eyes, looking at him in all black. Loyal wore a black vest over his black button-up shirt and a shirt collar tassel chain under his black necktie. His black wavy hair in a low-cut fade. His stubble of a beard was shaped nicely. He held a smile on his face. I couldn't help but admire how handsome he looked. I loved everything about this guy.

I wore a long black sleeveless dress with my right shoulder cut out. The left waist had a sleek cut-out and a sexy split, showing my mid-thigh. The dress was elegant and hugged every curve on my petite frame. My long hair was done in loose curls with the left side pinned back. I had his suit jacket wrapped around me, keeping me warm. The smell of his cologne lingered on the jacket, comforting me as if I were wrapped in his arms. I inhaled deeply, taking in his scent as I positioned my seat upright.

"How is it that you're not tired? I feel so drained." I said while stretching. I really did not want to leave his side. It was times like this that I wish we were living together. Apart of me was always sad when he left.

"I had to make sure you got home safely. I'm sure the tiredness will sit in when I get home." He said, looking around. "I guess we beat your parents' home."

"Or they're parked in the garage," I said, looking at the house.

"True! Well… let's get you in the house so I can head home." He said as he unbuckled his seatbelt. He got out of the car and walked around to open my door. He took my hand, helping me out of the car.

Loyal and I have been together for a little under a year and a half. I grew up with my dad constantly telling me how a man should act and how I'm supposed to be treated. I felt like the men that my dad would describe no longer existed. I dated a few guys, and none of them would come close to what my expectations were until I met Loyal. In some ways, he even reminded me of my dad.

On the other hand, my mom taught me how to treat and respect my man. We had so many talks while she taught me how to keep a clean house, pay bills, and cook. Even though she makes fun of my cooking. I haven't seen her turn down not one of my meals, not even my gourmet hamburger helper. I grew up watching my dad romance my mom and them running through the house like kids having water gun fights. Growing up in my house wasn't perfect, but it damn sure was close to it.

Loyal walked me to the door. After I unlocked it, I stepped inside, holding the door open for him to follow.

"Oh, it's cool, babe. I'm going to head home. I'll be back later in the morning to get the barbeque going, remember?"

"Oh yeah. I forgot that quick." I admitted, yawning while handing him back his suit jacket.

"It's alright. Go get some sleep. I'll text you when I get home."

"Okay," I said as he grasped my waist and pulled me into himself while he kissed me. His lips were soft and warm. I parted my lips slightly to allow him to slip his tongue inside. The mint taste from a mint he had earlier lingered on his tongue as he kissed me passionately before breaking loose.

"Love you. Lock the door behind me." He said as he walked out.

"I will. Love you too." I smiled as I closed and locked the door.

I avoided turning on the lights so I wouldn't have to come out of my room to turn them back off. I was so tired. I planned on throwing myself on the bed as soon as my dress came off. Looks like I'm sleeping in panties and a bra tonight. I think as my shoes made a click-clack sound on the hardwood floor.

I knocked on my parents' closed door as I passed by it. "Mom, daddy... I'm home." I said, hopefully loud enough for them to hear me.

I was in awe when I reached my room and opened my door. There were candles lit all around my room. Red and white rose petals were all over the floor and bed. A chair was draped in a shiny gold material with a blackboard propped up. "Oh, my God!" I screamed out.

I was frozen by the sight in front of me. I slowly walked into the room and sat my purse on the bed. I just stood there, taking in the view and enjoying the smell of candied strawberries in the air coming from one of the candles. Then, I walked over to the blackboard. It read: Good early morning, Brielle. Surprise! This is for you to discover what you mean to me and how much I appreciate you being in my life. That's right! I want to make a promise, so go to the room your dad calls his office. Before you move, press play, take a seat, and listen to the groove.

A small speaker was sitting next to the blackboard. I pressed play and took a seat on the edge of my bed. The song "Where Would I Be" by Kindred the Family Soul resonated throughout the room. I sat on the bed while I listened to the music. Silent tears fell from my eyes, but I held a smile while I clutched my pearls. I had forgotten entirely about being tired.

After the song ended, I walked down to the door at the end of the hall. I opened the door to my dad's office. Just like my room, I was met with candles everywhere. Rose petals on the floor led to his desk, holding two large bouquets of red roses. This room smelt of Vanilla. I closed my eyes and took a deep breath as I lived in the moment. Loyal knows I love the smell of Vanilla. Another chair was in the corner of the room, draped in gold. I picked up the blackboard and read the message. In this room, just use your feet. Your mom and dad's room are what you seek. Before you go, press play and take a seat. I pressed play on the stereo and listened to the voice of Johnny Gill singing 'You For Me' as I walked to the desk to take my seat.

After the song ended, I made my way to my parent's room. I opened the door to the exact same setup. The scent of candied strawberries was in the air. I couldn't stop the butterflies in my stomach. I was excited to hear Loyal's next message through the song. The way I felt at this moment made me yearn for him. I missed him desperately as if I hadn't seen him just moments before. I needed him in ways I have never needed someone before. I couldn't wait to throw my arms and legs around him. He was my addiction, and at this moment, I desperately needed a fix.

I walked over to the stand draped in gold in the corner of the room and read the blackboard. To receive everything so divine, please go to the living room and look behind the blinds. But until then, press play and unwind. I pressed play and sat on the bed, playing with the rose petals. The voice of Gerald Levert filled the room, singing 'Made To Love Ya.' I giggled, wondering who would pick up all these rose petals.

I slowly walked to the living room and turned on the light. I couldn't help but wonder where everyone was at. I walked towards my dad's favorite chair, grabbed the blackboard from against the blinds, and read the directions. Press play on the laptop, take a seat and listen to the beat. After the song, go to the room where cars go to sleep. I read out loud with a smile on my face. I set the board down, noticing a laptop on the glass coffee table. I open the cover and press play. The sound of R. Kelly's 'Forever' flowed through the speakers. The waterworks start up again as I sit on my dad's favorite chair.

I made my way to the garage. Once I opened the door, my hands covered my mouth immediately as I cried harder. The garage was transformed into an elegant room. The walls were draped in gold. Candles were everywhere, and a white loveseat was in the middle of the room. Two end tables on both sides of the loveseat held a bouquet full of red roses. Loyal was sitting on the couch holding a rose. Seeing him holding a rose and wearing his black suit made it look like he had stepped out of a magazine. He was so handsome.

"Oh, my God!" I say through tears as I walk over to him. "How did you…" I couldn't complete my question as I continued taking in all the beauty surrounding me.

Loyal got off the couch, approached me, and kissed me. He pulled me towards the sofa and sat me down softly, handing me the rose. I noticed my parents sitting in the corner with smiles and my mom with tears in her eyes. Uncle Glen, Aunt Sherry, and CeCe also witnessed one of the sweetest moments in my life. Loyal dropped down on one knee and removed a black velvet box from his pocket.

"Brielle, we have been together now for almost two years. During those almost two years, we have been there for each other through thick and thin. You complete me, and I realize that because I feel whole every time you're with me. I crave you when you are away from me. I yearn for the days that you can be the last person I see before I sleep and the first person I see every morning. I thank God daily for putting you in my path and life. I love everything about you and pray you feel the same about me. Brielle, I would like to ask you on this day, the first day of the year, would you do me the honor of being my wife?"

"Yes, yes… yes, I'll marry you!" I said through uncontrollable tears as he slid the ring on my finger. I couldn't take my eyes off him as he got up from his knee, pulling me up with him, and hugging me tightly as I cried, staring at my ring.

At that moment, it was just him and me in the room as we kissed. I glanced in the corner through watery eyes and saw them clapping. My mom and Aunt Sherry cried. Their mouths were moving, but I couldn't hear them. At that moment, it was just me and Loyal… my fiancé.

I woke up to the smell of barbeque, immediately making my mouth water. I look around my room and smile as the evidence of Loyal's love for me remains untouched. I look down at my finger, smiling as I admire the white gold princess-cut diamond ring on my finger. Glancing at the clock on my dresser, noticing the time I panic. It's two-thirty in the afternoon. I hate waking up late.

I rush to the bathroom to shower and brush my teeth. Checking the hallway before I dash back to my room. After shutting the door, I noticed a small silver gift bag with white tissue sitting on my bed that wasn't there before. The label read from husband-to-be.

The corners of my mouth rose as I opened the bag. Inside was a white shirt with gold writing that read I said yes! There was a picture of a diamond ring, with the diamond covered in rhinestones.

Twenty minutes later, I was dressed and ready to eat. I wore the shirt Loyal had given me with my blue cut-out jeans and white high-top sneakers. Luckily, my hair still looked good from yesterday, so I left it untouched.

I make my way through the empty house, pausing at the French patio doors and stare in astonishment. It's not a New Year's barbeque, 'it's an engagement party. I'm stunned as I stand there, not believing that Loyal is still throwing out surprises. There were round tables scattered around dressed in white tablecloths. Silver candle holders in the shape of a diamond ring on each table.

I spotted a table draped in gold with a white cake covered in gold drip icing sitting on top. The cake topper was a silver diamond ring. White and gold balloons placed throughout the backyard. Some of the white balloons had she said yes slogans on them. The setup was beautiful.

I smiled when I noticed Loyal's family and some friends. Ciera was dancing with Keon, and Jessica was stuffing her face as usual. I was startled when someone came and hugged me from behind. I relax when the smell of his cologne hits me.

"Surprise." He spoke softly in my ear.

"Loyal, you said it was a New Year's barbeque. This is clearly an engagement party."

"Well, it would have been if you had turned down my proposal." He says planting kisses on my cheek and neck. "I bought New Year's decorations too, just in case you said no."

"Why would you even think I would say no?" I asked, enjoying the feeling of him being near me.

"Damn, girl. I don't know. I have never been so nervous in my life. I had so many scenarios running through my head. I don't know what I would have done if you had said no. You would have cut me deep girl."

"I don't know why you would even think negatively about my answer. You know how I feel about you."

"Well… we honestly never talked about marriage. I know how you feel about kids, but I didn't know where you stood on marriage."

"Either way, I'm glad you asked. By the way, thanks for the shirt." I said, turning around. I took a step back, noticing his outfit. He wore a white shirt that read I popped the question in gold writing, blue jeans, and white sneakers. We were dressed alike. "Loyal!" I laughed. "You planned this too?"

"No. I just bought you the shirt. I didn't plan on you wearing blue jeans and white shoes." He laughed. "Damn girl, you gone have these people thinking I'm sprung."

"As far as I'm concerned, you are. So now, are you two going stand in here all hugged up, or are y'all going out there and enjoy your party?" My dad asked as he came inside from the backyard carrying a pan of ribs, chicken, and hot links over to the countertop. He sat it down and grabbed a bottle of his homemade barbeque sauce from the fridge.

"That smells good, daddy."

"I know, baby girl. That's my special sauce. I put my foot in it. Loyal, I don't care how good you think you can cook, but you ain't got nothing on these ribs, baby boy." My dad says, laughing with his chest poked out.

"Pops! That sounds like a challenge to me. Don't start nothing, won't be nothing, old man."

"You better believe you don't know nothing about these ribs!" My dad sang. "We can have a cookout if you want to. You gone fuck around and get your feelings hurt. This here gone have you questioning your whole life, young man. Y'all come on out here and mingle with y'all guest." Daddy said as he grabbed the pan and went back outside.

I peeked out the window again before going outside. It was a pretty good turnout for only family and a few friends. With all the excitement I've felt since coming home from the New Year's Eve party and the surprise engagement party, I no longer felt tired or sore from a night of dancing.

Loyal and I stepped outside, dancing to Bruno Mars's Finesse remix. Everyone started clapping and shouting out congratulations while joining us as we danced. After we finished dancing, Loyal's identical twin sisters, Honor and Justice, snatched me up.

"Hey, girls!" I said as I hugged both of them. I could not tell them apart if my life depended on it.

Over the past year, I have gotten very close to Loyal's family. Loyal told me the more time I spent with them, the easier it would be for me to tell them apart. That was the one and only lie he's ever told me. I spent more time with them and CeCe than I spent at home. Maybe it was the thousands of twin games they played on me. Even though I had difficulty distinguishing between them, CeCe always figured it out. Honor and Justice were my height, with golden brown skin and brown almond-shaped eyes.

Their hair was styled in short butterfly locs with golden brown highlights, which brought out their skin color. They were beautiful, but I hated when they wore their hair the same. I swear they did it just to mess with me. They were twenty-five years old with the same bubbly personality.

"Let me see the ring!" Justice said, grabbing my hand.

"He didn't even tell us he was thinking about popping the question," Honesty said, taking my hand from Justice.

"Really?" I asked, shocked that they didn't know.

"That's because you girls can't hold water," Trust said, coming up from behind me. "Hey, lil sis, congratulations." He said as he hugged me.

Trust was the eldest brother of the twins and Loyal. He was dark-skinned and was the spitting image of his father. He was as observant as Loyal and very overprotective. Still, when he relaxed with a couple of drinks in his system, he knew how to party.

"Thanks," I said, hugging him back.

"You let me know if he starts acting up. I'll straighten his ass out for you."

"Not before I do." My dad said, coming up to me out of the blue. He patted Trust on the shoulder and gave him a smile. "Hey, baby girl, your mom is looking for you."

"Alright, thanks," I replied as I looked around the backyard. I spot my mother talking to Loyal's mom. I closed my eyes and took a deep breath as I walked to her. This party was going to be tougher than I thought. Being pulled from one person to another just to be congratulated was exhausting.

CHAPTER 4

Brayden

Two more weeks I think to myself as I admire my handy work. I pulled on the metal bars I put over the window from inside the room. I honestly didn't need to add the bars. The window was so small, wasn't anybody coming in or out of that bitch. I just liked the way it looked with the bars on it.

Falling back on the mattress I'd just thrown on the floor, I took a look around the basement room of my new house. This room was perfect. Luckily for her, the bathroom was attached to the room otherwise, I would have just given her bitch ass a bucket. I tugged on the chains on the floor near the mattress to ensure they were secure to the bolts on the wall. There were chains hooked near the top and bottom of the mattress.

There was a mini fridge in the corner of the room that I just finished stocking with a pack of lunch meat. One pack of bologna, nasty ass shit, even I don't eat that shit. That's all the fuck she gone eat though. She's lucky I even got her ass some bread.

I got up from the mattress and grabbed a bag off the floor. I unwrapped the blanket and the sheet and tossed them on the mattress. Grabbing two water bottles, I placed them on top of the mini fridge. I gathered the trash and turned the light off.

Before leaving the room, I turned around, taking in Ciera's new room. It's bright in here, I thought. "I'm going to have to change that shit. I don't need that bitch counting fuckin days and shit. I have to block that window. Man Mason… I wish you were here to see this shit." I say out loud as I close the door.

I walked through the rest of the basement and up the stairs. "Shit," I said as I patted my pants pocket, looking for the padlock. I shrugged it off as I grabbed a tall metal rack and slid it in front of the basement door before walking out of the pantry and shutting the door behind me. When this house was built, I made sure to add a basement with a hidden door. I spotted the padlock on the sink as I walked out of the kitchen. I'll remember to grab it when I go back down next time.

As I strolled through the kitchen and living room, I couldn't help but admire the empty house. It's a nice fuckin house if I do say so my damn self. Too bad I'm not on that family bullshit. This is the perfect house for a family that's just starting to grow, friendly ass neighborhood and shit. I have to be careful. I already had three mother fuckin people ring my damn door talking about some welcome to the fuckin neighborhood. One person had the nerve to bring some damn green bean casserole. I thought they only did that shit on tv. I know damn well I don't look like no casserole type nigga. If you want to welcome a nigga; you better bring me a bucket of chicken… shit. Thank goodness, I made sure my windows were soundproof. I don't need these nosey ass people knocking on my door in case they hear that bitch scream.

I walked to the backyard, grabbed the tarp left by the builders, and stuffed it in front of the small basement window. I also spotted a bin left behind and dragged it in front of the window, ensuring the tarp didn't blow away. I didn't want any light coming into the window. This isn't the damn Hilton', she's not about to enjoy this stay.

After putting everything in place, I walk through the house, ensuring everything is locked up. I head to the garage and hop into my new black-on-black Dodge Durango. This bitch was so new it didn't even have tags, which was perfect for when I carried out my plan. I backed out of the garage and waited for it to close before taking off. I had a one-hour drive back to Diamond Watch Securities.

I ended up taking a detour when I got back to the city. I drove slowly past Gerald's house and noticed their asses were back there partying. The double iron gate was wide open. I could clearly see Keon's dumb ass hugged up with Ciera, and Gerald was behind the grill with a big ass grin on his face talking to Glen and some other nigga I ain't never seen before. Looking at them made my blood boil. I felt nothing but pure hate for their entire family. I put up a middle finger and speed off toward the office.

"These mother fuckers over here enjoying themselves too much. I'm about to wipe the smiles clear off their fuckin faces, and I can't wait. I got you, Mason."

CHAPTER 5

Glen

I got to hand it to Loyal. This was a fine little turnout. I didn't expect this many people when he said it was just family and a couple of friends. Loyal had a big ass family compared to our little family of three. This is my first time being around Loyal's family. I could tell Gerald and Brenda were comfortable with them. They talked as if they had known each other for years. I sat at the table, taking in the scenery while nursing my Budweiser. Lil' Kim's Not Tonight was blasting through the speakers. Loyal and Brielle were on the dance floor, along with Jessica and Loyal's brother Trust, his sisters Honor and Justice, and some other friends I wasn't familiar with.

I watched how well Brielle interacted with Loyal's family. If I didn't know her, I would say she was born into that family, with how close she was to Loyal's sisters and brother. Looking around for Ciera, I spot her hugged up with Keon, taking selfies. I shake my damn head at her. That girl is forever taking pictures. Sherry was off with Brenda and Lisa, Loyal's mom. It's crazy how much Lisa reminds me of Brenda. They say everyone has a twin. I guess Brenda found hers. Lisa had a medium brown complexion; she wore her long black hair straight with bangs and wore blue jeans and a black hoodie.

I got up and headed over to Gerald. I had something important I needed to discuss with him. "You got it smelling good overhear G!" I yelled over the music.

"You know how I do, baby boy. I don't play when it comes to my grilling."

"Don't you think you got more than enough food out here?"

"This is the last batch." He said as he brushed the food with his special sauce.

"Hey… Can I speak with you for a moment in private?"

"Yeah… um… let's go to my office." He answers, taking off his black Grill Master apron. He looks around before setting his sight on Loyal.

"Loyal!" He yells over the music.

Loyal pulls himself away from the group and jogs over. "What's up, Pops?"

"Hey, I gotta run in the house for a moment. Can you keep an eye on the grill for me?"

"Sure, no problem."

"Here, put this on so you don't mess up your clothes." He says while handing Loyal his apron. "I don't want Brielle nagging at me about mess'in up your outfit."

Loyal takes it slowly from Gerald, folding it across his arm. "That shouldn't be an issue." He says slowly as he focuses on something behind me.

I turn around, looking behind me. The side iron gates were wide open, giving me a full view of the house's front. All I see is the tail end of a black SUV driving by.

"The shirts were my idea." He says, giving us his full attention.

"What!" I laughed. "The shirts were your idea? Be careful, once you start that shit, they gone always expect it." I said, taking a swig from the Budweiser bottle I was holding.

Loyal smiled and held both hands up as if he was surrendering. "Hey, what can I say? That's wifey right there."

"Not yet. Brielle's still my baby girl. Listen, I'll be right back. Don't burn my food or try to find my secret ingredients, or I'll have to kill you." Gerald said, turning to walk away. I follow behind him.

"I can't make no promises, sir!" Loyal yelled back while poking at the food on the grill.

"Yeah, but I can!" Gerald yelled back, laughing.

I followed Gerald to his office. There was a black wall storage unit that covered the whole back wall. In the middle was a black picture that said Make Your Move. There was an arrangement of books, picture frames of the family, and trophies neatly on the shelves. The trophies were from the different fighting competitions he's won. Off to the side of the window was a small black table with a fancy black and gold chest set on top of it, and two black chairs pushed into the table. An L-shaped black desk with a glass top sat at the other end of the office. On the same wall next to the door sat a black loveseat.

This was the only room in the house decorated with gray brick wallpaper. It really made the black in the room stand out. I was shocked when I first saw it. Brenda and Gerald were both partial to the color blue. Walking through their home, you'd know their favorite color. They never overdid it; it was always just the right hue for each room.

"Hmm, I see you didn't waste any time taking down them gold decorations from Loyal's proposal," I said while still looking around.

"Hell naw. I didn't want him using this room in the first place. Brenda made me do it."

"Yeah? How did she do that?" I said, grabbing my laptop case from the loveseat and sitting at Gerald's desk.

"She threatened to renew our vowels."

"No! She took it there, bro?" I laughed.

"Yeah, she's been having wedding fever ever since Loyal came to us about marrying Brielle a few weeks ago. I love my Brenda, but that was a one-time thing. Hopefully, she gets this whole renewing our vows idea out of her mind once she's done helping Brielle plan her wedding." He says, taking a seat in his chair.

"I hear you."

"So, what's up? What did you need to speak with me about? You got me in my office, so it must be serious." Gerald asked, leaning back in his chair behind his desk.

I grabbed two folders from my bag and tossed them on the desk before Gerald.

"What's this?" He asked.

"A while back, when Ciera first brought Keon around. I decided to do checks on him and thought hell, I might as well do one on Loyal too. So, in addition to our normal background checks, I did some underground digging. You know, you can't be too safe nowadays. Anyway, they just came back." I said.

"Damn, bro… after a year, you're just now getting them back?'

"The normal checks came back a while ago. They were clear. It's the underground checks that took the longest. Supposedly, some info was hard to come by."

"Did something pop up?" He asked, skimming through the paperwork for Keon.

"Check out the shit that pulled up about Keon's dad."

Gerald's eyes got big as he read the report. "Wow!"

"Now check out Loyal's dad," I said as I opened Loyal's report and gave it to Gerald.

He read the information and sat both papers side by side, comparing the documents. He nods his head, "Yo, this is crazy!"

"Right!" I said, agreeing with him. "Just think… if I hadn't done these checks, we would have never known because them lil niggas ain't said shit. Both of them have been around for a little over a year now. They could have told us." I said, slightly irritated at the secrecy.

"Do you blame them? What are the odds of this happening? Both of their fathers. I wonder if Keon and Loyal knew each other before meeting our girls." Gerald said.

I could tell his mind was working. He was rubbing the stubble on his chin and nodding his head slowly. His eyes were going back and forth between the documents.

"Do you think they purposely went after our girls? What if this is a setup to take us down." Gerald asked.

"Take us down? We have a legitimate business. They have no reason to come for us… I believe they genuinely love Ciera and

Brielle. Plus, we never had any quarrel with their fathers… so, what do you think we should do?" I asked.

Gerald leans back in his chair, crossing his arms over his chest. He was silently thinking. I knew he was in deep thought. These reports were in no way to be taken lightly. I knew the weight of the information when I gave it to him. Their fathers were dangerous men. If this information ever got out, it could also be dangerous for Loyal's and Keon's fathers. It had the potential to put our daughters in danger. I took a deep breath and tried to think things through. We could break them up, but I don't want that on our conscience.

"What do you think we should do?" He asked me the same question I asked him.

"I don't know, man," I said, shaking my head. I don't know where to go from here because now we're dealing with matters of the heart. I can't tell Ciera to stop dating Keon, and Loyal is now engaged to Brielle."

"I agree," Gerald said, flipping through the paperwork again. "You know, according to the dates. It looks like they may be retired." He said as he handed me documents from both Loyal and Keon.

"Looks like no movement in the past three years," I admitted.

"Honestly, I don't think we have anything to worry about. Those young men out there love our girls, and not to mention Loyal's dad already seems protective over Brielle. He treats her as one of his own. As a father, I couldn't ask for more."

"So, you're not worried?"

"I'm always worrying. We know firsthand how dangerous this world is, but I also know Loyal would never do anything to harm Brielle. The same goes for Keon, he's infatuated with Ciera."

I nod my head in agreement. "So, what do we do?"

"I say we do nothing," Gerald says, leaning back in his chair.

"Well, do you at least want to bring them on, see if we can find a place for them at Diamond Securities?" I asked.

"Bring who on exactly?" Gerald asked skeptically.

"Their fathers, hell, Keon and Loyal too."

"Man, have you met Loyal's father? If not, that man is right out there." He said, pointing to the window. "That nigga smells like money, and from the looks of his information that pulled through on Loyal's report. He is not looking for employment anytime soon. I'm sure the same goes for Keon's father. Someone in his position can't just switch jobs. Have you met him yet?"

"Yeah, a few times. Well, what about the boys?" I asked.

"No. If they want to work at Diamond Securities, then fine. But as of right now, it doesn't look like they're trying to get with us either. They're doing their own thing."

I sigh. Gerald was right. Maybe I'm overthinking this whole thing. Ciera and Brielle are my babies, and it pains me to know that they are involved with people who have an extensive family history. Yet nothing tells me that Keon and Loyal can't be trusted.

"Here," Gerald says, gathering all the papers and placing them back inside the folders. "You should put these in the safe. We don't want anyone to stumble across these."

I grab the folders and walk to the bookcase. I removed the Make Your Move picture from the wall and pressed my palm to the safe, unlocking it. Gerald and I were the only ones that could get into the safe.

"Do you think we should tell the girls?" I questioned.

"No, this is something you don't want everyone to know. That's probably why Keon or Loyal haven't told the girls. Hell, they could have at least told us, they know what we're about. Let's keep this information among ourselves in case something ever pops off. We can use them as a last resort."

"Alright. Aye, what if Ciera and Brie already know? Has Brielle hinted anything to you?" I asked curiously.

"No, I would remember some shit like this, and she would know to come to me with information like this if she knew. Has Ciera said anything about Keon?"

"Nope. Then I guess it's safe to say they don't know." I answered.

Back outside, we noticed the party had calmed down. Everyone was grouped up at separate tables. The women were all seated at one table with three bottles of wine in the middle of the table and a wine glass in front of each of them, along with a plate of food.

Whatever was going on, I could tell they were happy. There was a smile on each of their faces. I also spotted a pen and paper on the table as I walked by. The men were grouped together at a table behind the women. I noticed the table they were sitting at wasn't an original table that was out when the party started.

"I know like hell y'all not over here playing Goldfish on my poker table," Gerald said, sounding insulted. "Look at this disrespectful shit." He said, backhanding me in my chest.

"Naw, Mr. G. We just out here keeping the table warm until y'all got back. We didn't want to start the game without you." Keon said, laughing.

"No problem, son. Let me pull up a chair so I can teach y'all something." Gerald said, taking the deck of cards.

"Naw, forget teaching. I'm about to take y'all money." I said, pulling up a chair.

"Hey Nathan, this is my brother Glen. Glen, this is Nathan. Loyal's father." Gerald said, introducing us.

"What's up?" I said, giving him a nod.

"Nice to meet you." He replied as we gave each other a fist bump.

"These two are Loyal's friends. This is Chris, and that's Trey." Gerald said, pointing at the two young men sitting at the center of the table.

"How y'all doing?" I greeted them.

"Hello, Sir." Chris gave a respectful nod from across the table.

"Nice to meet you." Trey greeted, reaching out his hand to shake mine.

"Damn, so what happened? It looks like the battle of the sexes out here. One minute, everybody was dancing and mingling. I leave and come back, and everyone is separated. What happened?" I asked as Gerald started shuffling the cards.

"Man… the women started the 'Wedding talk' before we knew it they were huddled up planning the wedding," Loyal said.

"Umm…. Loyal, don't you think you should be in that conversation?" Gerald asked.

"Nope. Brie will let me know what I need to do. Just tell me the date, what to wear and where to be. This is her day, and I'll do whatever I can to make her day special. She knows, we already talked about it.

"It's a big day for you too, son," Nathan said, patting Loyal on the shoulder.

"Hey, didn't I leave you at the grill?" Gerald asked.

"Yeah. It's done. I didn't see any more meat left out." Loyal answered.

"Yeah, that was the last batch. Alright!" Gerald says, shuffling the cards. "Texas Holdem, ante up five dollars. Who's in?"

☐

CHAPTER 6

Ciera

Two weeks later

I woke up to the sound of Run the World (Girls) by Beyonce. I slowly opened my eyes, staring at the ceiling while listening to the beginning words of the song. "Alexa, stop the alarm!" I shouted out with an attitude. As if Alexa could tell I was irritated by her waking me up. I was not happy to leave the comfort and warmth of my bed.

Today was my first day back to school from our long winter break. These have been the busiest two weeks of my life. Brielle's and Loyal's wedding planning started the day of the engagement party. Since then, they have picked a date and put a deposit on a venue. From what I hear, Loyal's parents and Brielle's parents are going half on the cost of the wedding. But honestly, I already knew money would not be an issue. So far, the wedding party has already been chosen. It's been so fun hanging out with all the women. In addition to my mom and aunt Brenda, Lisa, Honesty, and Justice tagged along too. All dresses and accessories have been picked out with the exception of Brielle's wedding dress. The wedding is scheduled to take place at the end of the year, November 30th.

I'm excited for my cousin. This is definitely her year, a double celebration: graduating with her bachelor's degree and starting a new life with Loyal.

I jumped at the sound of my phone vibrating on my nightstand, interrupting me from my thoughts. I reached for my phone and smiled when I saw the person's name ringing me.

"Good morning," I sang into the phone, hoping my voice didn't crack.

"Hey sexy, you up?" Keon asked. I could hear his smile in his voice. Keon was a morning person. He had an infectious enthusiasm for life that I found inspiring.

On the other hand, I was not keen on early rising, but hearing his voice in the morning always put me in a pleasant mood. I was amazed that no matter how late he got to bed, he always woke up early with energy and an optimistic attitude. I was curious to find out his morning routine so I could potentially incorporate it into my life. Maybe he was meditating, exercising, or reading something inspiring to start his day. Whatever it was, I needed to learn more about it and try it out.

"Yep, just in bed thinking about my day. I don't feel like going to school today." I said, yawning.

"I know, but it's gotta be done. What time is your first class?"

"At eight thirty, then math at ten o'clock."

"My first class is at nine. Do you want me to pick you up?" He asked.

Keon went to Red Canyon University with Brielle, Loyal, and me. He majored in criminal justice, and only had one year left before graduating with his master's. I have so much fun with them at school that I hated to think of the days I would have to attend school alone. I was three years behind everyone since I started school late.

"No. That's alright. Though I would love to spend extra time with you. I have work today. I'm going to head to Ami's after my last class." I sighed.

"Oh. Well, 'let's do lunch after our second class. You get out at eleven, right?"

"Look at you! Over here memorizing my schedule. Yeah, it's over at eleven." I smiled.

"Hahaha," he laughed sarcastically. "My second class ends at eleven-thirty. Meet me by the student center at Tonya's Tray for lunch."

"Ooh, you read my mind. I've been craving some salt and vinegar fries and hot wings. So now that I got something to look forward to let me get off this phone so I can get dressed. I've wasted too much time laying in this bed."

"Well damn… That's how you really feel?" he asked, sounding insulted.

"What?"

"You look forward more to eating hot wings and fries than to seeing me." He laughed. "I'm beginning to think our relationship needs some work."

"Yeah well, at least I can count on the wings and fries to be there when I need them," I giggled. Keon knew how I felt about him.

"Wait until I see your ass at school, girl," he threatened sarcastically.

"Well, I guess I'll see you soon." I chuckled.

"Alright then, later Ciera." He replied before hanging up.

I smiled at him, calling me by my first name. That usually meant I was in trouble, but his form of punishment could end with an unwanted pregnancy if we weren't careful. I didn't even want to think of all the drama that would cause. My parents were old school. Marriage first, then the baby carriage.

I jumped out of bed, quickly showered, and brushed my teeth. I didn't feel like getting dressed today, so I wore light blue jeans, a white Canyon University hoodie, and black tennis shoes. I quickly put my hair in two cornrows, going straight back. I laid my edges and put on my small white gold hoop earrings.

I planned to head out the moment I was done dressing since I was already pressed for time, but the smell of bacon diverted me to the kitchen. I walked into the L-shaped kitchen. There were black cabinets with white marble countertops and a matching backsplash of white marble.

My mom was standing in front of the kitchen window rinsing out a dish. She wore black and white plaid pajama pants, a black tank top that stopped just above her belly button, showing off her flat stomach, and her pink bunny slippers. Her hair was in a messy pineapple bun, that poked out of her dark blue scarf that was tied around her head. She had a cinnamon-colored skin tone like me. She turned around and looked at me as I sat my backpack down.

"Mornin' Pumpkin," My mom said with a smile. "I knew I would catch you before you left. You have time to eat?"

"Not really. I could take it to go instead." I said as I looked at the spread she had made.

"Here's your plate. Stack it up and make you a sandwich to go."

"Thanks, mama," I said as I grabbed the plate of eggs, bacon, and toast. Then, I started building my sandwich.

"You work today?" She asked as she handed me a sandwich bag.

"Yeah. My last class lets out at two. I start work at four. What about you?"

My mom worked part-time as a registered nurse at Hope Memorial Hospital. She didn't need to work but would much rather spend some of her free time helping others instead of being cooped up at home most of the time.

"No. I don't work today. However, I will be meeting up with Brenda today. We're shopping for Brielle's and Loyal's wedding gift." She said as she fixed her and my dad's plates. Looking at their plates made me wish I had more time. She really went all out this morning. She fixed her famous banana nut pancakes, eggs, bacon, and hashbrowns.

"Isn't it a bit early to be shopping for a wedding gift? I asked, still eyeing her plate.

"You would think so, but this must be purchased in advance." She smiled.

"Dang, mama! Why did you make pancakes on the day I had to leave early for school? Your timing is horrible. Can you save me some for later?" I asked as I picked up the carton of orange juice from the counter and poured myself a glass.

"Nope!" My dad yelled from behind me, startling me. Causing me to spill a little juice on the counter.

"Daddy!" I shouted. "You scared me!" I said, slightly irritated.

He then reached over, took my glass, and downed the remaining juice in three gulps. I punched him in the arm. My dad was so ripped most of the time it didn't seem like he would even feel my hits. He had on gray sweatpants with no shirt.

"Really daddy! Mama! I yelled, calling for her to come to my aid.

"Glen, Here... take your plate and leave that girl alone. She's already running late for class."

"That ain't my fault." My dad said, smacking my mama on her ass.

"Ah... but you're contributing to my lateness by stealing my juice and having me clean up after the mess you caused," I said, cutting my eyes at him. I could tell my dad was in a playful mood this morning. Usually, I clown around with him, but today was not the day.

"You mean the orange juice that I bought with my money?" He quizzed.

"Yep," I said, popping the P sound as I poured the last bit of orange juice into my glass and quickly drank it before he tried to beat me to it.

"Oh! You're being a little smartass this morning. How many pancakes are left babe?" He asked my mom as he stuffed some food in his mouth.

"Three," she replied.

"Not anymore!" He said as he turned towards the griddle, looking around. "Wait... where are they at? I thought you said there were three left?" He asked, confused.

"Not anymore!" Mom laughed, handing me Tupperware with my pancakes and a fork. She even packed me a little container of syrup.

"Haha" I laughed. "Thanks mommy!" I said, grabbing the Tupperware and kissing her on the cheek.

"Sherry! You're supposed to be on my side, woman."

"I guess she loves me more." I giggled as I kissed my dad on the cheek.

"You may have won the battle, but…."

"I won the war too, daddy." I laughed, cutting him off. "Love you guys. I'll see you later." I said as I walked out of the kitchen.

"Love you too!" They say in unison.

"Be safe." My mom added.

"We need to talk woman, bring your fine ass over here." I heard my dad say just before I heard the sound of them kissing, causing me to shutter Thank goodness I was on my way to school.

I arrived at school with five minutes to spare. Thank God I found a parking space near the humanities building. I made it to my anatomy and physiology class right on time. Professor Adams was known for locking the door. He did not tolerate tardiness. Which I thought was ironic, given how slowly his tubby ass walked. He was an Italian man with curly gray hair. He actually had a cuteness to him if it wasn't for his round physique and gray hair. However, this class was taught by two professors at the same time. Mrs. Hawkins taught alongside Mr. Adams. Her blond hair, slim build, and funny personality made her stand out. Even though Mr. Adams was older, he was still vibrant and full of life. His wit and energy kept us all engaged and looking forward to his class. Mrs. Hawkins was a stark contrast to Mr. Adams, youthful and energetic, yet just as wise.

I loved listening to Mrs. Hawkins. She was so raw, she talked about how she and her husband decided to relocate from Minnesota to California because oral sex was illegal. She then moved to Arizona because of a job opportunity. Once she was settled, she found out that oral sex was illegal here too. She plans on moving back to California once her contract is up.

Mr. Adams talked about how it's like that in the military also. Supposedly, oral sex is illegal, and the only sexual position you can do is missionary. I'm thinking to myself... who in the hell would tell? Some of these crazy state laws make no sense to me. Mr. Adam's favorite thing to do was put on pornos and explain what was happening, as if we couldn't see it for ourselves.

After class ended, I gathered my things and pulled out my phone. I was headed to math which started at ten, so I had thirty minutes to burn. I planned to go to the math building and start my homework until class began.

I left the humanities building behind a few students who had just left the classroom. I noticed a person standing against the wall wearing black jeans and a black hoodie. I couldn't see the person as their hood was pulled over, and their head was down while they fiddled with their phone.

I dialed Brie's number and was about to press the call button when I felt something hard poke me in the back. I inhaled sharply. "What the hell!" I yelled; I was about to turn around when an arm was thrown over my shoulder.

"Shhh, you yell, you get a bullet through your back."

My heart rate immediately spiked, and my palms began to sweat. The ominous words rang through the air, leaving me feeling a chill of fear. I could feel a sense of dread and fear enveloping me, my body tensing up as I took in the gravity of the situation. I stopped walking and looked straight ahead.

"Who are you? What do you want?" I whispered.

"Don't worry about that right now. Who did you call?" he whispered back.

I was so nervous I couldn't think. I was too scared to do or say anything. He shoved the gun harder into my back.

"I asked you a question. Who did you call?" he repeated.

I looked down at my phone, realizing the number was still displayed. I didn't hit the call button. "Nobody," I answered, holding up the phone so he could see it.

"Good. Walk to your car and act normal." He whispered.

I tried my best to walk casually to my car. My vision was blurred by tears that threatened to fall. I looked at people as I walked by, praying they would read my expression and know that I needed help. I was scared. My heart was pounding, and I felt like I was walking in slow motion. I could barely breathe. Nobody even bothered to make eye contact with me. I frantically scanned the parking lot, hoping to spot Keon. That was short-lived after I remembered his class started at nine. It was already nine-thirty.

I found the courage to speak as I walked over to my car's driver's side door. "I need to get my keys out of my backpack."

"No, you don't. Get your phone and throw it on the ground." He demanded.

I did as he said, and he kicked it under my car.

"Now open the back door of the truck parked next to you."

I looked to the left and noticed the black SUV parked beside my car. I opened the door slowly.

"Now slide inside. Move slowly. No funny business, and don't think about running away. The doors won't open from the inside."

I felt a chill go down my spine as I carefully and slowly slid inside. Once inside, I started to turn my neck to get a glimpse of who was kidnapping me, but before I could look at him, he quickly grabbed my head, tilting it to the side as he pushed something sharp into my neck. I yell out as I feel an intense burning sensation before everything turns black.

CHAPTER 7

Keon

I was hoping CeCe would have taken me up on my offer to pick her up. That would have been my excuse to get to school early, locate my classes, and stop by the bookstore to get items I was without. I hung up the phone, disappointed. I don't know what it was about that woman, but I just couldn't get enough of her. I know I used to tease her about being the future Mrs. Wright. The more time I spend with her, the more I realize she might be. Especially since this is the first woman my mother approves of, and my dad already feels he has two daughters now. I smile, thinking about the attitudes they give me when I visit without her on my side.

I yawned and stretched my arms as I sat up on the side of the bed. I grabbed my phone off the bed and searched for my hip-hop playlist. As soon as Drake's Money In The Grave' started blaring through the Bose speakers in every room of my condo, I stood up and then dropped to the floor to do my thirty-minute morning workout before hitting the shower.

I worked my way through push-ups, sit-ups, and planks. I made sure to throw some weights around before calling it quits. The entire time of my workout, my mind raced about CeCe and everything I wanted to do to her. By the time my playlist ended, I was dripping with sweat. Afterward, I quickly showered, dressed, and whipped up a protein shake before rushing out the door.

My morning was moving slowly. I showed up to my first class and was greeted by a locked door and my classmates waiting in the hall patiently for the instructor's arrival. After waiting fifteen minutes, I grabbed a sheet of paper wrote down the class name and my instructor's name along with the time I arrived and signed my name. Luckly one of my classmates had tape, I taped the paper to the door and walked out but not before noticing the line of people waiting to sign their name.

My Juvenile procedures class flew by fast. Before I knew it, the professor assigned us a research paper due next week. He announced that we were open to partnering up if we wanted to and dismissed the class. When he said we could work with a partner, I saw Leilani turn around and give me a smirk. I continued looking at the professor but noticed Leilani in my peripherals. It was difficult not to notice dark brown almond-shaped eyes staring at me. Her black hair with red highlights slicked back into a curly ponytail with bangs that stopped below her eyebrows.

I noticed her when she sashayed her skinny but curvy ass into the classroom and sat down in the third row. She wore a red short-sleeved shirt, white shorts, and red slide-in Sketchers. Leilani was my ex. I learned the hard way that she wasn't a one-man type of woman. Leilani had a natural beauty that the opposite sex couldn't ignore. She was manipulative and used her beauty to get what she wanted. But I learned my lesson and cut off ties with her the moment she broke my trust.

I got up and gathered my things quickly. I wanted to leave before she made her way towards me. Leilani was relentless. I thought she finally got the point of leaving me the fuck alone when I wouldn't answer her calls. Six months after I got with CeCe, Leilani spotted us hanging out with Brielle and Loyal just after a game of laser tag. She had the nerve to introduce herself as an old friend. The attitude and look she gave CeCe was a dead giveaway that she was more than a friend at one point. Ciera didn't miss a beat. As soon as Leilani walked away, she turned to me and asked. "Is she someone I need to be worried about?"

"Hell no!" I answered, bringing my mouth to hers.

I made my way to Tonya's Tray and was surprised when I didn't see Ciera sitting at the patio table. Before taking a seat, I stepped inside the restaurant to see if she was waiting for an order. I was ready to tease her for being too greedy to wait for me. The thought of her in line waiting for her order had me grinning as I searched for her. To my surprise, she wasn't there either. I called her phone; it rang a few times before going to voicemail. Her last class finished thirty minutes before mine. She should have been here by now, I thought.

I shrugged it off and decided to wait for her outside at our usual table. Different scenarios started to flash in my mind as to the reason she would keep me waiting.

I stared at people walking around for a bit before starting some homework. I had nothing else better to do since I wasn't hungry. I had only decided to meet CeCe here because it was one of her favorite places to eat on campus.

"Hey, Keon!" I cringed at the voice as she sang my name. Her voice irritated me instantly. "You mind if I sit here?" Leilani asked, interrupting me from my work.

I looked up to see her standing in front of me. "Yes, I do, actually. I'm waiting on my woman." I said, trying not to sound as irritated as I felt.

"Your woman!" She uttered, then rolled her eyes. "Well, I won't take much of your time. I just wanted to ask if we could be partners on our assignment?" She asked as she played with the necklace around her neck.

"No. I work alone." I said dryly.

"Well, can you at least help me with it?" she pouted.

"If you were paying attention to the instructor instead of watching me all the damn time, maybe you would've understood the assignment."

"Oh! So, you noticed me?" She smiled as she took a seat.

"I notice a lot, and yo… That wasn't an invitation to sit your ass down. If my woman saw you hitting on me-"

She crossed her arms across her chest. "What! Princess afraid of a little competition? Why you over here acting like we don't have a past? Don't you miss me?" She asked, leaning over the table and reaching out to caress the side of my face.

I quickly smacked her hand away before she could touch my skin. "Aye, keep your nasty ass hands off me," I stated.

I was getting more annoyed each time Leilani opened her mouth. I glanced at my watch. CeCe was almost thirty minutes late this wasn't like her at all. She would have texted or called if something came up.

I started packing up my things. "Leilani, one important thing you should know about me is that I don't go backward. My past is exactly what it is 'the past.' You don't get a second chance, especially after catching you in bed with my pops."

Leilani smacked her lips. "I already apologized for that. I didn't know that was your dad." She whined.

"You expect me to believe that, with all the family pictures you've seen at my crib? Regardless of who you opened your legs for, you still cheated. And I don't give second chances!" I yelled out. I was frustrated partly because of Leilani's trifling ass and the fact that I was worried about CeCe. "Listen…" I said, trying my best to calm down. "It's been what… two years since we ended. It would be best if you stopped pushing up on me. I've moved on. If Ciera finds out that you're still com'in for me, I won't stop her from giving you the ass whopping you deserve." I said, getting up and tossing my bag over my shoulder.

Leilani rolled her eyes. "Ain't nobody scared of her bougie ass. She has something that belongs to me."

"If you value the way you look, fall back Leilani," I said as I walked away.

"I don't know why you're so worried about her anyway. She stood you up, so she can't possibly care about you that much. Where are you going? I still need help with the assignment!" She shouted.

"Figure it out your damn self!" I yelled back as I redialed CeCe's phone number and waited for her to pick up.

You've reached Ciera. Sorry, I missed your call... I groaned as I ended the call. I got a feeling in the pit of my stomach that something wasn't right. The one thing my pops taught me was to always listen to my instincts. I rechecked the time. I had just under an hour until the start of my next class. I dialed Brielle's number as I walked to the humanities building. Thankfully, she answered on the second ring.

"Hi Keon, what's up?" She answered, her voice hoarse as if she had just woken up.

"How are you doing Brie? Sorry for waking you?"

"No problem. I was getting up anyways. What's up?"

"Have you heard from Ciera or seen her?"

"No. Today's my late day. My class doesn't start till twelve. Is everything okay?"

"Uh… She was supposed to meet me for an early lunch. She never showed up." I said as I was steadily looking around the campus as I walked.

"Maybe she had to stay after class," Brielle said. Her voice was strained from talking in the middle of a stretch.

"That's what I was thinking. Alright, I'll see you around." I didn't want to tell her that it's been almost an hour since she was supposed to meet me or that her phone was going unanswered.

"Alright, bye." She said, hanging up the phone.

With every second, the dread I felt in my stomach got worse. I went from a fast-paced walk to a quick jog. I burst through the glass door and ran up the stairs. I spotted Mr. Hawkins locking the door with his briefcase in his hand.

"Hey… Mr. Hawkins!" I shouted as I approached him. Not caring about the other classes nearby that were in session.

"Ahhh!… Keon, my former student. How can I help you?" He asked, speaking just as slowly as he walked. It took everything in me to be patient with him.

"Can you tell me if Ciera Taylor made it to class this morning?" I asked as calmly as I could while I approached him.

"Ciera Taylor," he repeated her name as he thought about it. "Yes, she was," he said, nodding his head. "She barely made it on time, but yes. She was in my 8:30 class this morning. Is everything okay?" He had a concerned look on his face.

I sighed in relief at hearing that she had made it to school. The relief was only short-lived because that dread feeling came back and had me haul ass to her math class. "I hope so, thank you!" I shouted as I made my way back down the stairs.

I stood there, staring at the door as Mr. Gibson closed the door in my face. It seemed as if everything was moving in slow motion. The only thing I could hear was the rapid beating of my heart. I stumbled backward, hitting my back against the wall. My breathing was labored, and I started seeing blue dots floating around. I slid to the floor, dragging my hands down my face. "Come on, Keon," I whispered to myself. Taking a few deep breaths, I slowly rose to my feet. Pull yourself together. Get up! I urged myself. I stood up slowly, still leaning on the wall. "Shit!" I whispered to myself as I kicked myself from off the wall. I dashed out of the building and called Glen. The phone rang and was sent to voicemail. I hung up and immediately called Diamond Securities.

"Diamond Security, this is Kim. How can I direct your call?"

"Is Glen in?"

"Yes, he is. To whom am I speaking with?"

"Keon"

"Okay, Keon. One moment while I transfer you." She said just before the line went silent. The next voice I heard was Glen. The sound of his voice actually made my heartbeat faster.

"Hello," he greeted.

"Mr. Glen-"

"Hahaha," he laughed, cutting me off. "Boy! What's up with all this, Mr.? You make me feel old. Call me Glen."

"Mr. G." I continued, ignoring him. "I can't find CeCe."

"What's up young man? You can't keep up with these young ladies?" he laughed.

"Naw, Mr. G. You're not understanding me right now. Something is wrong. She was supposed to meet me for lunch but never showed up. I called her several times, and no answer." I replied, standing in the courtyard, praying that I spotted her.

"Well, maybe she had a meeting after class or something. Are you sure she's not giving you the silent treatment?"

I thought for a moment that maybe she was upset if she'd seen Leilani flirting with me. But then again, CeCe isn't the type to just walk away without letting her feelings be known. So, I quickly pushed that thought out of my head.

"No. We didn't have any argument." I answered.

"Maybe she went to the restroom. Don't get yourself worked up Keo-"

"Mr. Taylor!" I yelled, cutting him off. "With all due respect, sir. The current time is 12:15. I was supposed to meet with CeCe at 11:30. I waited thirty minutes with no calls or texts from her. That's not like her."

"Well, perhaps-"

"Mr. G!" I yelled, interrupting him again. I don't know if this man is in denial or if he's just not hearing me. "Listen, I spoke to her 8am professor, he said she made it to class. Her 10 a.m. professor said she was absent today. She only made it to one class."

The phone was silent. I took the phone from my ear and looked at it to make sure the call didn't get disconnected. Then I put the phone back to my ear.

"Hold on a minute, son." He said as he put the phone down. I could hear him messing around with something in the background. "Keon, you there son?" he asked, getting back on the phone.

"Yeah, I'm here."

"Okay, give me a sec. I'm pulling her location up on GPS."

"Alright." I sighed, running my hand through my hair. I crossed my arms and waited. My patience was wearing thin. I couldn't shake the feeling that we needed to get moving. Too much time had been wasted.

"So, it shows here that she's at school. I tried calling her too, and it went to voicemail. Listen here Keon, I know how you feel about my daughter. Now you're saying you have a weird feeling something is wrong. Im'ma need you to lead with that and give me something concrete because from where I'm sitting, she's safe at school. Maybe she forgot to take her phone off silent or even lost her phone. Nothing so far screams that she's in danger, so let's not jump to conclusions until we have all the facts."

"Dammit!" I grunted through gritted teeth.

How the hell is it that I know his daughter better than he does. CeCe lives through her phone, as many selfies she takes throughout the day. Ain't no way she lost that phone, but I didn't want to argue with this man. If he wanted proof, then I needed to give it to him. I quickly glanced around my surrounding area one last time from where I stood, trying to think of something, anything that could prove CeCe was in trouble. To me, missing a class and not texting or calling if she can't meet up is evident enough. I know my woman, and regardless of what anyone else says this wasn't like her.

I refused to wait until nightfall for someone to realize she was missing. Time was of the essence. I subconsciously started walking towards the humanities building.

"Alright Mr. Glen. You said, per the GPS, her car is in the parking lot, right?" I asked.

"Yeah, though I'm not sure which parking lot."

"Not a problem," I remember her professor saying she barely made it to class on time, which meant she was running late. She would have tried to find the closest parking space to her class. Stay on the phone with me. I'm almost to the parking lot."

Glen took a frustrated breath. "Alright." He said.

I walked down the first three isles before I found a red 2021 Hyundai Sonata. I quickly walked to the side of the car and checked the front passenger and driver's seats for the red cherry seat covers that CeCe loved. "Found her car," I stated as I continued to walk around the car, looking for any signs of a struggle or damage.

"Are you sure it's her car?" Glen asked.

"Yeah, the cherry-covered seat covers are a dead giveaway. The plate number is BVX2428."

"Yep, that's her. How does the car look? Any damage?"

"No, it's fine. Aye, can you call her number again? I want to see if she left her phone in the car."

I don't know why I asked him to call her number. I doubt it was left in the car. Not only would she have gone back to retrieve it, but she also would have made it in time to meet me. I don't know if I hoped it would ring for my comfort or Glen's. I still had a feeling that something wasn't right.

"Give me a sec… Okay, it's ringing." Glen said.

We got quiet as we listened for the phone. Almost immediately, I clearly heard a phone ringing. It wasn't muffled as if it was inside the car. I started following the sound, getting low to the ground.

"Is that her phone?" he asked.

"Yeah…" I confirmed as I bent down. "But it's not coming from inside the car." I spotted the phone on the ground behind the driver-side rear tire. I reached under the car to grab the phone. "Her phone is under the car… and it's cracked." I stood up, holding CeCe's phone, staring at it in disbelief.

My phone went silent as I waited for Glen to speak up. Ciera would never drop her phone and leave it there. My mind started coming up with different scenarios as to what could have happened to cause her to leave her phone.

"Mr. Glen, I think Ciera may have been abducted… What do you want me to do?"

The silence on the other end of the line weighed heavily on me. Anger and fear gnawed at me, making it difficult to think clearly. I knew we had to act quickly but didn't know where to begin.

Finally, Glen's voice broke the silence, his tone grave and serious. "Stay there. I'm on my way."

☐

CHAPTER 8

Glen

I'd just finished speaking to Keon and hung up the phone with unsteady hands. I couldn't believe what I'd just heard. My day had been great so far, and now my world had been turned upside down within minutes. My stomach was in knots as I tried to process what Keon had just said. My eyes scanned around my office, noticing the few pictures that hung from the wall, my eyes lingering on Ciera. Then I caught sight of the single shelf on the wall that held a few of Ciera's trophies she'd won over the years. I also looked at some of the trinkets she made me for Father's Day when she was little. I thought back to the day she gave me one.

I was lying on my bed streaming a game on the NFL network On Father's Day morning. Sherry had woken up early to fix breakfast and forbade me to get out of bed before she served me. She walked into the room carrying a tray of food, and right behind her was four-year-old Ciera. She looked so cute, her hair brushed in two long pigtails and wearing her red and black polka dot pajama set. I remember those being her favorite pj's because they reminded her of Micky Mouse. Ciera followed behind her mother, her shoulders hanging low, and her bottom lip poked out.

I asked Sherry, "What's wrong with her?"

She gave me a soft smile and replied, "Ask her." As she placed the tray on the nightstand.

I looked over at Ciera, telling her to come to me as I held my arms out. I lifted her on my lap and looked into those sad green eyes. "What's wrong, Muffin? Why do you look so sad?"

"I made you a present for Father's Day, but it didn't come out right." She pouted.

"What!" I shouted out in excitement. "You made me a Father's Day gift?"

"Yeah, but it's not right." She whined. She looked like she was on the verge of tears.

"But I still want it. I'm sure I will love it anyway because my Muffin made it for me."

"Okaaay…" She said, dragging the A sound as she held out her little hand, handing me a clay object. It was green, flat, and round. The edges were raised slightly on one side. It fit snugly in the palm of her hand. "It was supposed to be a bowl, but it's not. And that in the middle is supposed to be a heart, but it looks like a broken circle." She whined as she explained her gift to me.

There was blue paint in the middle. It did look like a circle with a dent in it. I smiled as I took it from her.

"I knew that was a heart," I told her.

"You could tell?" She asked with a smile on her little face.

"Yeah, it's beautiful. You know Ciera… I'm going to make some people really jealous with this gift."

"Why?" she asked with a confused look on her face.

"Because I'm the only person with a half bowl. Nobody else can get one because my Muffin made it for me. I will put it up in my office so everyone can see it." I smiled.

"You really like it?"

"Yeah, I love it. Thank you so much for making this for me." Then I whispered in her ear, "Your mom could never make me a gift as beautiful as this one. Don't tell her I said that." I smiled.

Ciera laughed and jumped into my arms, throwing her small arms around my neck and squeezing as hard as her little body could.

"You're welcome, Daddy." She said, with all the sadness in her voice gone.

I let out a chuckle that brought me back to reality. My eyes landed on a photo on my desk of Ciera hugging me at the beach. I grabbed the picture frame, dragging my fingers against the glass, wishing I could feel the warmth and softness of my baby girl's cheek. I felt like I was in a trance as I recalled the day we took that photo, the memory still fresh in my mind.

The picture was taken four years ago at a beach in Nassau, Bahamas. It was a hot day, the sand was white, and the turquoise water made you feel like you were standing in the middle of a postcard. Ciera decided her loving embrace was her most effective way of begging me to parasail with her. Sherry thought Ciera's pouty lip and big, rounded green eyes were the funniest thing ever and hurried to snap the picture. Ciera knew I couldn't deny that look. I finally conceded, and we spent the next thirty minutes parasailing over the crystal clear waters and taking in the beautiful scenery. I screamed my ass off the first ten minutes but afterward enjoyed it.

There was a knock at the door that caused me to look up. My brain was so far gone I didn't know what to say in response to the knocking. The doorknob turned, and Gerald's head poked through the cracked door. When he noticed me sitting at the desk, he took that as an invitation to walk in smiling.

"Good news Brah! You know that account we've been trying to get for the past three months? Global Dynamics." he continued without me answering him. "Zuri just hit me back. They want to sign." He exclaimed.

I could only stare at him as I heard everything he said. It was definitely good news. But I felt numb to everything, including my emotions. I stared at him, hoping he could hear my cries for help. I needed help, yet here I am, a grown-ass man. I can't even find my damn voice.

"Aye, Glen... You alright, man? You look as if you just saw a ghost."

"Ah...ye...yeah," I clench my eyes shut and shake my head, trying to get my mind right. "I mean, no. No, I'm... not okay." I replied slowly, I knew I was speaking, but I could barely hear myself. I had to concentrate on the words I was trying to say.

"What's going on, man? I'm not used to seeing you like this. You're scaring me." Gerald said as he took a seat in front of my desk. "You feeling okay, man?" he asked.

"Ciera needs help... my ah... my baby needs me. Something happened. I have to... I need to go." I stood up, patting my beige cargo pants pockets for my keys. I wore a white graphic Tee and started patting my waist as if I had pockets on my shirt. I glanced at my desk, looking for my phone and keys as I patted myself down. "I can't find my phone. Where are my keys? Pocket... they're in my jacket pocket." I turned around, looking for my jean jacket.

"Glen!" Gerald yelled as he snapped his fingers, causing me to turn my gaze toward him. "What's going on, man? All I heard was Ciera before you started mumbling." He stood up.

"I- I... I need my phone." I stuttered.

"Your phone is lying right in front of you, man." He said, pointing to my phone on my desk. "What's going on? Talk to me, dammit!" he shouted, clearly getting frustrated with me.

"I- I.. don't know. Keon... he called and said Ciera might be in trouble. She's missing."

Something about saying it out loud snapped me back into reality. I fell onto my chair hard, my emotions causing my heart to break. I fought hard to stop the tears. I knew I needed to be strong, but I felt like part of my soul was being ripped from my body.

"I- I can't think, man. I don't know what to do. That's my baby girl!" I shouted.

"Shit! Give me your phone," he said, holding out his hand.

I picked up my phone and pressed my thumb on the sensor, unlocking the screen as I handed it to him. He scrolled through, then put the phone to his ear.

"Keon! This is Gerald. Talk to me."

Gerald stared at me as he listened intensely to the voice on the phone, giving an occasional nod or an "uh huh." I placed my arms on the desk, lacing my fingers together tightly as I pressed my thumbs together, trying to relieve some of the anger I was now feeling. Once I find out who touched my daughter, whoever it is just signed their death certificate. I thought. I couldn't wait to get my hands on the son of a bitch.

"No, I'll be there in ten. I'll meet you in front of the office. Do you have my number?" Gerald's words brought my attention back to him. "Good! Do me a favor. Call me so I can save your number... Sure, see you in ten." He stated before disconnecting the call.

His phone immediately starts to ring, and he silents it before handing me back my phone. I reached for my phone; my leg was shaking uncontrollably. All I felt at the moment was fear and anger.

"That's my daughter, brah… my heart!" I grunted. "I need to do something, man. Tell me what to do. I don't know what to do." I cried.

"Glen … right now, I need you to call the police and Sherry. Im'ma go meet up with Keon, review the security footage, and see what I can find out."

"Damn man, how the hell am I going to tell my wife that her daughter is missing?" I said through clenched teeth after slamming my fist down on my desk.

This is not a conversation that I ever planned to have with my wife. My heart was already broken, knowing my daughter might be scared, hurt, or even dead. Breaking my wife's heart was the last thing I ever wanted to do. I swear when I get my hands on the person responsible for this, I'm gonna expose their inner organs to daylight.

"I understand how you feel, Bruh, but this isn't something that you can keep from her. She's bound to find out, and it's better if she hears it from you. She's going to need you and you her. Get her here now and call the cops. Im'ma head down to the campus, and I'll call you to let you know what I find out." He slapped the back of my shoulder and rushed out the door before I could utter a response.

I sucked in air through clenched teeth as I dragged my hands roughly down my face wiping away my silent, angry tears. I dialed Sherry's number. I felt my heartbeat faster with every second that the phone rang. I urged myself not to break down on the phone with Sherry. Gerald was right. I needed to be strong. I knew Sherry was out house shopping with Brenda, and I said a quick prayer, thankful she wasn't alone. Sherry answered the phone laughing, and I also heard laughter in the background.

"Hey boo, what's up?" She giggled.

I could hear the smile on her face when she spoke. Knowing I was about to turn her day upside down broke me down even more. I bit down on my tongue hard, hoping the pain would somehow keep me from breaking down while I spoke.

"Babe!" She repeated. "Did you butt dial me again? Glen!" She shouted while laughing.

"I'm… I'm here." I uttered with a wavering voice. There was an awkward pause as I tried to find the right words.

"what's up, babe?" She asked again.

"Umm, I…" I closed my eyes as I filled my lungs to capacity. "I need you to come down to the office, babe."

"Sure, I'll come by later when we're done. I think we have three more houses to view."

"No, sweetheart, that won't work."

"What, why, Glen?" She whined. "You know Brenda and I have been planning this for a while. What do you need me for? Isn't Gerald there?"

Hem hem, I cleared my throat. "Something came up."

"What came up?"

"There's been a situation. I need you to come to the office asap. Bring Brenda with you."

"Situation! What kind of a situation?"

I dragged the phone away from my ear, letting it rest near my chin. I squeezed my eyes shut as I took another deep breath, bracing myself to tell this woman news that no parent ever wants to hear. Anger and fear poured through me again as it took everything in me to hold it together. I banged my fist against the desk.

"What was that sound? Glen, you're scaring me." The happy tone she greeted me with was now laced with worry.

"Ciera may have been taken."

"What do you mean she may have been taken?"

"Our baby is missing… she may have been kidnapped Sherry," I spoke in a broken voice as I wiped the tears.

"No… no… no. Not my baby Glen. Ciera!" She screamed. "Is this some type of sick joke?" she sobbed. "Why would you tell me something like this? This isn't funny Glen!" She screamed through tears.

"No, baby, I would never joke about something like this."

My voice cracked even more. I'm not even sure she heard me. I wanted to comfort her, but what could I possibly do for her over the phone? I just wanted to hold her, but I knew my presence alone wouldn't be enough to soothe her soul right now. But at least I would be there with her, reminding her that she was not going through this alone. I made out Brenda's voice in the background, asking what's going on but getting no answer from Sherry.

Sherry was hysterical, crying and screaming, "Not my baby." I heard a quick shuffle, then Brenda's voice came through the phone.

"Hello, Glen. What happened? What did you say to Sherry?"

"Brenda, please… Can you get-" I sighed, removing the phone from my ear, trying to calm myself down. I felt like shit over here, crying and losing my damn mind. I've taught Ciera well. She can defend herself. My daughter and wife needed me, and I needed to be strong. I took a deep breath and put the phone back to my ear. "I'm sorry. Brenda, listen I need you and Sherry to get to the office asap. Ciera may have been taken."

"Wait, what do you mean by taken?"

"She may have been taken against her will, as in kidnapped."

"How, when?"

"I'm not sure about the details just yet Brenda. Gerald is on the way to the school to view security footage."

"Wait a minute, Glen. Don't you think you're jumping the gun a little? If you don't know any details, what makes you think she's been kidnapped? For all we know, she could be in class."

"I pray you're right Brenda." I sighed. "In fact, I thought the same thing. However, Keon did some investigation on his own, and things are not adding up. Gerald will be calling me soon with info from the video footage. In the meantime, I need to call the police. Can you please-"

"Yeah, do that. We're on the way." Brenda interrupted me, panic visible in her voice before disconnecting the call.

Thirty minutes later, my office has been turned into an interrogation room. I'm sitting in a chair, holding Sherry while she sits on my lap. We are surrounded by three police officers. I can feel sweat dripping down my forehead as they ask me questions I don't know how to answer. My heart is pounding in my chest as the tension in the room and the frustration grows with every passing minute. I notice the officers exchanging glances, and I can see the disbelief in their eyes as I answer their questions. I'm struggling to keep my composure and I know Sherry can sense my anxiety.

"So, all you can tell me, Mr. Taylor, is that Ciera left your house just a little past eight this morning. She made it to her eight-thirty class but didn't make it to her ten o'clock class. Her phone was found under her car, and she wore light blue jeans and a white hoodie." Officer Mallard confirmed as she looked at her notepad.

She stood tall in her navy blue uniform, and her rust-colored hair was slicked into a tight low bun. She was petite yet curvy with pale skin. Her freckles bought out the color of her hair. She held a look of compassion as she periodically looked at the pictures of Ciera hanging around the office.

"As of this time, that's all I know," I answered with a slow nod.

"Mr. Taylor, you're not giving us much to go on. I mean, for all we know, she could have dropped her phone and-"

"What Officer Levi is trying to say." Officer Stanley said, walking towards my desk as he interrupted Officer Levi. He gave him a warning scowl as he approached me. Officer Levi raised both hands, indicating he'd back down. "Is that we normally like to get started on a missing person's case as soon as possible as you know, time is a critical factor in these cases. You mentioned earlier that Gerald went to check the security footage. Can you phone him to see if he's found any additional information?" He asked, his deep voice taking a softer tone than Levi's.

Officer Stanley was an older white guy with a receding hairline. He stood about six foot four, maybe even five, and had an I don't take no shit type of attitude, and from what I hear from the other officers, he can back it up.

I glanced back at Officer Levi. He seemed like he had better things to do than to be here. Tensions were already high, and that smug look he kept on his face made me want to knock his fuckin head through the wall. Officer Levi was the shortest person in the room. He looked like he was dressing up in his navy blue uniform. I'm glad Officer Stanley stepped in when he did. I thought to myself as I reached for my cell. A knock at the door caused Sherry to jump.

"Glen!" Brenda shouts as she rushes into the room. "Gerald is on line one. He's been trying to call your cell, but it goes straight to voicemail." She said as she picked up the call and put the desk phone on speaker. "Gerald bae, everyone is here," Brenda spoke.

"Gerald! Please tell me you got something?" I pleaded.

"Yeah, so Ciera walked out of her first class at nine-thirty-five. Her attention was on her phone while she was walking from class. A person wearing a black hoodie and dark blue jeans was posted outside her class. It looked like he was waiting for her."

"Can you see who it was?" I questioned, hopeful.

"Was it Keon?" Sherry asked.

"No. It's definitely not Keon. Whoever it is, I can't see the face." Gerald replied.

"Well, if you can't see the face, how do you know it's not Keon? As of now, he's still a suspect until we can prove otherwise." Officer Levi said.

I shook my head. "Naw, man, it definitely isn't Keon. He loves Ciera. If it wasn't for him, we wouldn't even be aware of her missing right now."

"That means nothing. Keon could have ulterior motives." Officer Levi smirked.

. "Yo, man, what's your fucking problem?" I yelled as I grabbed Sherry's waist, lifting her and standing her up beside me. I strolled towards Levi as Sherry pulled on my arm. Her attempt at holding me back failed. I was ready to take my anger out on someone, and Officer Levi would do just fine. "I done had enough of your sly ass remarks with your Napoleon fuck'in complex. You got a problem with me and mine? Cause if you do, I can handle you right here and now." I shouted.

"Mr. Taylor. You don't want to do this. He's an officer!" Officer Mallard bellowed as she took a stance before me, pushing me back.

"I don't give a fuck who the hell he is. Lil nigga you come'in for the wrong one. You better watch how you speak to me…"

"Mr. Taylor, please… have a seat." Officer Mallard said, pushing me back and down onto my chair. "Let's focus on getting your daughter back."

"Officer Levi! You are out of line. Do you need to be removed from this case?" Officer Stanley asked.

"No, sir."

"Well, another negative outburst like that, and I just might let Mr. Taylor school you in the proper way to speak to people." Officer Stanley stated, obviously tired of Officer Levi as well.

"I'm sorry sir, I'm just stating the obvious. I didn't mean no disrespect." Officer Levi said through clenched teeth.

"Didn't mean it my ass," I grunted as Sherry took her place back on my lap.

Officer Mallard leaned over my desk, speaking into the phone. "Sorry for the interruption, Mr. Taylor. Please continue. Did you see any weapons?"

"Yes, a gun. He points it at Ciera's back the moment she walks past him. She never saw it coming." Gerald replied.

Sherry gasped, and my stomach dropped at the mention of a gun. My heart raced as I imagined Ciera's fear at that moment. I felt helpless, knowing I couldn't do anything to help her. My mind raced with possibilities of what could happen next, but I was powerless to do anything. I shut my eyes and silently prayed for her safety.

"What happened next?" I asked.

"He has her walk towards his vehicle, which was parked conveniently next to hers. She tossed her phone on the ground towards her car just before being forced into his truck. Also, we noticed a little struggle coming from him, and after slowing the clip down, we noticed a syringe was pulled out of his pocket. It looks like he drugged her." Gerald said through clenched teeth.

After hearing his last words, my body drooped in my chair. Sherry started shaking on my lap as her silent tears turned into loud sobs. Brenda had both hands covering her mouth as she cried silently. I just sat there, numb and motionless, unable to fully process what I had just heard as I felt my own tears start to fall. I was supposed to protect my daughter. But here I was, part owner of a multimillion-dollar security company, yet unable to keep my own daughter safe from harm. Powerless to help her as her world came crashing down.

"What's the vehicle description?" Officer Stanley asked.

"Black Dodge Durango. Looks like a newer model."

"Please tell me you got the plate number?" Brenda pleaded. She stood on the opposite side of me, caressing my back.

"No, the truck had no plates." Gerald sighed.

"Dammit!" I yelled, as I slammed my fist down onto my desk. "Can you at least see the direction they turned out the parking lot?"

"They made a right, but this parking lot only exits right. So that wouldn't be much help. Oh yeah! Ahh…Officer Levi, just to let you know, I have already checked the security footage referring to Keon's timeframes. His alibi checks out. He was in class at the time of Ciera's abduction." Gerald stated.

I eyeballed Levi's punk ass in the corner of the office. He shrugged his shoulders as if he didn't care. Levi got up and walked out of the office without saying a word. I didn't trust him.

Officer Stanley spoke into the phone. "Mr. Taylor, this is Officer Stanley here. Can you get a copy of the footage you viewed?"

"Yes, a copy was made for me."

"Great! Can you send a copy my way as well? I'd like to review the footage myself. Two sets of eyes are better than one."

"Yeah, I'll get it to you."

"Thanks buddy. Mr. Taylor," Officer Stanley said, returning his gaze to me. "We'll keep in touch. Let me know if anything else comes up."

"I will," I tell him before he turns around to walk out the door. "Officer Stanley! I don't want Levi on this case."

He stopped and turned around, giving me a long, serious look. Then nodded. "Understood." Then left my office.

Officer Mallard gave a nod as she followed behind him. I leaned back in my chair as I rubbed Sherry's back. I felt uneasy about Levi. I trusted Officer Stanley and Mallard, but I couldn't shake the feeling of dread in my stomach.

"Gerald, how's Keon doing?" Sherry asked, breaking the silence in the room.

"Not good. I sent him home a while ago." He huffed. "We wouldn't know none of this right now if it wasn't for him," Gerald admitted. Brenda nodded her head in agreement.

"He loves Ciera just as much as Loyal loves Brielle," Brenda said. I nodded my head. More than you know, I thought to myself. "Oh, my God! How are we going to tell Brielle that Ciera is missing?" Brenda gasped; her cheeks wet with tears.

"Let's not tell her until she gets home tonight," Gerald said.

"That's if Keon hasn't called her or Loyal yet," Sherry mumbled.

"Alright, y'all. I'm on my way back. I'll see you in ten." Gerald said before ending the call.

We sat in silence, each lost in our own thoughts. Mere minutes seemed like hours. My stomach churned as I felt a wave of numbness wash over me. I couldn't believe this was happening. I couldn't focus on anything. I felt like I was in a nightmare and had no control over the situation. Sherry leaned her head on my shoulder.

"Do you think they will find our baby?" she asked.

"I hope so. We need to stay positive, babe." I replied, holding her close. I peeked at Brenda as she swabbed tears from her eyes.

She whispered, "I don't think they have enough information."

I don't know if Sherry heard her, but I did and silently agreed with her. I just didn't want to say it. I stared at the picture frame on my desk again. I felt the urge to do something. I couldn't sit here while my baby was out there, afraid for her life. I tapped Sherry on her ass. "I need to go for a ride. I'll keep a lookout for a black Dodge Durango." I said, standing up.

"I'm coming with you." Sherry insisted.

"You guys go ahead. I'll wait here for Gerald. I'll let you know if we hear anything." Brenda sobbed.

"Thank you sis," I said, giving her a quick hug before rushing out the door with Sherry close behind me.

☐

CHAPTER 9

Brayden

I arrived at the house and watched as the garage door closed behind me. I'm surprised I pulled this off as effortlessly as I did. The first part of my plan went down smoothly, but there was still much more to do. Two things will drive a man crazy: his family and his money, and I plan on taking both away from Glen and Gerald. With my plan in motion, I had to be careful not to get too complacent. After all, I still had to ensure that Glen and Gerald didn't catch wind of my scheme, or else all my hard work and planning would be for nothing. I was confident they wouldn't know what hit them until it was too late. It was time to get to work.

I peeped at CeCe from my rearview mirror just in time to see her turn her head as a moan escaped her luscious lips. I hurriedly got out of the car, snatched the door open, and gave her another shot in the neck, more than what I had previously given. I didn't expect her to wake up so soon. I still had another errand to run, and I did not want her to wake up until I returned. Worst case scenario, she dies from an overdose. That wasn't my plan, but I could live with that.

I pulled her out and tossed her over my shoulder. I carried her downstairs to the basement, flung her on the mattress, and shackled her wrists and ankles. I tightened the chain, ensuring not to give her too much room to move. I turned the lights off and locked the door before walking back upstairs. I quickly changed into a brown tracksuit and my black Nike hi-tops. Snatching a couple of slices of cold pizza out of the fridge and stuffed my face as I walked to my car and hopped into my Infinity.

I headed to Diamond Security, claiming that there were forms I was late in filling out when in reality, I was just anxious to see the look on Glen's face when he found out that his precious daughter was missing. Due to Ciera's busy schedule, there's a good chance he won't find out she's missing until tonight. I thought as I shuffled my hip-hop playlist. Tavis Scott's Sicko boomed through the stereo as I backed out of the driveway. Usually, I hate going to the office, but today is the beginning of a great fuck'in day!

The number of police cruisers in the parking lot shocked me when I arrived at the office. It wasn't a lot, but it was definitely more than the few that generally show their faces around here daily. I spotted my co-worker, Vic, walking out the door as I approached.

He was one of the most down-to-earth white guys I ever met. He wore a black tank top, beige cargo shorts, and some damn black thong sandals. The way Vic was dressed, you would think it was summer and not the middle of winter. I gave him a nod. "What's up, Vic!" I smiled, raising my arm to meet his fist bump.

"Damn Bro! It's been a minute since I saw you up here on your day off. What brings you to headquarters?"

"I was in the area and thought I'd stop by… fill out some paperwork I've been procrastinating on. Know what I mean? What are you doing here? Last I heard, you were in Boston." I asked with a nod.

"Man, the Townsend contract is up for renewal. They're doing renegotiations, so while they are busying themselves with the formalities of the contracts, I got me a temporary gig in New York."

"Oh yeah! How temporary?" I asked.

"Three days. I'm going to head back to Townsend once the contract is renewed. They know how to treat a brotha up there, ya now?" Vic laughed.

I knew very well what he was talking about. The Townsend contract was among the highest-paid contracts. In addition to great pay, the guard's uniform included a few pairs of Armani suits, a tux, black sunglasses, a couple of high-end casual outfits, and an assigned Lincoln Navigator. Twenty guards were assigned to the company, each with their own condo. The Townsend smelled of money and ensured their workers held the same scent. If I weren't so caught up in getting revenge on the Taylors for my brother's death, I would have definitely tried to get in with Townsend. "Yeah, man, I know what you mean." I laughed. "Yo, what's going on with all these cruisers?" I nodded toward the police cruisers.

"I'm not sure. They were here when I pulled up. Something about a missing person. Probably a client issue. It wouldn't be the first time."

"Are they in there with the Taylors?" I asked.

"Glen. Gerald left a while ago." He answered.

"Alright then, let me get up in there and handle my business," I uttered as I gave Vic a pat on the back.

"Yeah man... I'll see you around."

"Bet, I haven't forgotten I still owe you that ass whipp'in" I yelled as he walked off towards his car.

"You can try if you want to. You remember what happened the last time we were in the ring." He yelled back, flipping me off without turning around.

The smile left my face as I entered the building. I was curious to know why the police were there. They couldn't be here regarding Ciera. It had only been four hours since I took her. I wasn't expecting them to notice her missing until tonight when she didn't return home from work. Either way, it wouldn't bother me if it was regarding Ciera. I made sure not to leave any clues as to who I was. I smirked, knowing that even if they did have leads, it would lead them straight to a dead end.

"Hello, Brayden." The receptionist said. The sound of her voice took my attention away from my thoughts. "What brings you up here on this fine day?" She asked while stuffing envelopes.

"Hey Kimmy, I need-"

"You know I hate it when you call me that. It's Kim or Kimberly, fool." She snapped, folding her arms across her chest, her eyebrows squeezed together in an irritating frown.

Kim was a thick, rounded woman and carried herself extremely well. Her taste in fashion made her look sexy as fuck. Every outfit she wore showed off her voluptuous curves. Her short hairstyle somehow accentuated the roundness of her face, making her more beautiful than I thought she should be, at least for someone I wasn't attracted to. Kim wasn't the type I usually mess with. I loved dark-skinned beauties with natural hair, no matter how skinny or thick. Kim was light-skinned with a short strawberry-blond weave and constantly wore too much makeup, but something about her made me want to dip in her garden.

"I'm sorry, Kim, I forgot." I lied. I loved to see her frown. Her attitude made her even sexier. "I need some forms."

"You know all forms can be done online." She said through pursed lips, obviously still upset with me calling her Kimmy.

"Yeah, I'm aware… I'm just old school. I'd rather fill them out and file them myself." I smiled.

"Alright." She sighed. "What forms did you need?" She asked, getting up from her chair. As much as I wanted to see her walk away in those tight-ass jeans, I stopped her.

"Naw Ma. Don't get up. I know where they are. I'll get it." I offered.

"Are you sure?"

"Yeah, "I said, nodding my head.

"Okay, it's on the shelf next to Glen's office. Check the file cabinet to the left if you don't see what you need in the tray." She said, pointing towards the hallway.

"Thanks," I said as I walked to the shelf, thankful Glen's door was open.

I took my time flipping through the different paperwork as I listened to the conversation that was taking place inside Glen's office. I couldn't help the smile that formed on my face. They indeed knew that Ciera was missing, and just like I'd planned, they had no idea who'd taken her or why. I didn't mind if they knew about my truck. I'd received my plates in the mail a few days before but refused to put them on the car. I rolled around with no plates, and kept the car parked in the garage.

I could hear the irritation in their voices when they concluded they didn't have enough details. I fought to hold back my laughter, especially at the sound of Glen's helpless ass. I was confident that the authorities would be stumped. I had planned this out well. They had no chance of cracking this case. I felt a sense of satisfaction knowing that I had outsmarted them all. I laughed as I walked away, wishing I could see the pain on Glen's face.

"Later, Kimberly!" I said as I passed her desk.

"Hey, you heard Mike is back?" Kim asked.

I couldn't help but notice the happiness in her voice at the mention of his name. I shuddered at the thought of him. Mike was a tough dude, and his physique made him intimidating. I sparred with him several times, even though I got a few good hits I couldn't take that nigga down if my life depended on it. If I ever crossed him, I knew the only way to beat him would be to take his life. Mike was also Glen's right-hand man. Why the hell is he back? It can't be a coincidence that he decided to come back on the day I took Ciera.

"Is his contract over already?" I asked Kim.

"I guess so. It was supposed to be for two years, but I guess there was a change in plans." She shrugged. "It would be nice to have him back?" she smiled.

"Hmm," I murmured, shaking my head. Glen had to call for Mike's help, that weak ass nigga. This couldn't be a coincidence. Nobody leaves a client before the agreed-upon date. I thought to myself. "Well, catch you later," I said, trying not to sound as dry as I did. I was out the door before Kim could respond.

☐

CHAPTER 10

Ciera

"Ugh…" I groan in frustration as the throbbing in my head begins. I slowly opened my eyes and found myself staring at the ceiling of a dark room. The pounding in my brain was now accompanied by a sharp pain in my eyes, causing me to let out another moan of discomfort. It felt like I had a headache in my eyeballs, an odd sensation that left me wondering if such a thing was even possible.

Desperate for relief. I closed my eyes once more and turned my head to the right. As I did so, I felt a stiffness in my neck, adding to my growing discomfort. The combination of a pounding headache, eye pain, and neck pain made it clear that this was going to be a difficult day. I gasped when I realized my bed wasn't facing the right direction. The disorientation intensifies as I recall being kidnapped. The thought sends a chill down my spine, and my stomach drops with fear and dread.

As I jolt upright, a scream escapes my lips. It wasn't until this moment that I became aware of the restraints that confined me. My heart was pounding in my chest as I examined my wrists and ankles, only to find them bound by cold, heavy metal shackles. The weight of the metal dug into my flesh.

"You're awake!"

I jumped at the sound of the voice. The fact that I wasn't alone had never occurred to me before. Uncertain of where the voice came from or who it was, I looked around frantically until he flipped the light switch on, causing the pulsating pain in my head to throb ten times worse. The sudden bright light in the room made me immediately shield my eyes with my arms.

"I was beginning to worry I might have overdosed you." He laughed.

I slowly opened my eyes to the figure sitting backward on a chair in the corner of the room facing me. He wore a brown tracksuit, sneakers, and a black ski mask. As I stared at him, I quickly tried to devise an escape plan. He looked like he weighed no more than two hundred pounds and couldn't have been much taller than me. I knew I could take him down. I just had to play my role and get him to trust me enough to take these shackles off.

"Whoever you are, please let me go. I don't know who you are or where I am. I swear I won't go to the police." I pleaded as calmly as I could.

"Oh, I know you won't."

"So... you'll let me go?" I asked, hopeful.

"Not a chance." He laughed.

"What do you want from me? Why did you take me?" I asked in a shaky voice. I refused to let him know I was scared as I fought to blink back my tears.

"You're asking too many questions." He teased.

"And you're not answering enough of my questions." I snapped.

He laughed. "Hold up Ma, you got the game all wrong. You don't get to ask questions. Your only job is to stay your pretty ass down here until I say otherwise." He stated.

I looked around the room, noticing for the first time that I was in a bedroom. By the looks of the small window sitting high on the wall, it might even be a basement. "If you want me to stay quiet, you need to answer something."

He chuckled. "You can make all the noise you want Ma. Ain't nobody going to hear you."

I sighed, feeling both frustration and fear. "Well, can you at least tell me how long you plan to keep me down here?"

The silence hung in the air for a moment, making me aware of the impending uncertainty. "Until I'm ready to let you go." He got quiet as his eyes scanned me up and down. The intensity of his stare sent shivers down my spine. "Who knows, I may even decide to keep you to myself." I could hear the smile in his voice.

I rolled my eyes, not wanting to show the fear I felt. I tried to gather my thoughts. I decided against pleading with him. It was apparent pleading wasn't going to get me anywhere. I held up my shackled wrist, waiving it in the air. "'It's obvious that I'm not going anywhere. Can you at least unshackle me?"

He sat up straight, crossing his arms across his chest. "Ground rules. First, no screaming. This is a soundproof room, Not that anyone would hear you, it's just that I don't want to hear that shit if I'm around. Secondly, you stay your ass in this room. You try to come out; you remain shackled for the duration of your stay. Do you understand?" He asked sternly.

I rolled my eyes. "Yeah, I got it."

"The bathroom is right there." He said, pointing to the left. That mini fridge has some sandwich meat in there. If you get hungry, make yourself a sandwich. There's bottled water if you get thirsty." He pointed to the mini fridge on the side of the mattress. There was a loaf of bread sitting on top of it. A case of bottled water sat on the floor next to the fridge. "If you're good Ma, I may even bring you a treat. Any questions?"

"Yeah," I held up my wrists. "Can you unlock me now?" I asked dryly.

He stalked over to me, pulling a chain of keys out of his pocket. He kneeled down and unlocked my ankles first, then my wrist. "I don't want no trouble, or things could get much worse for you Ciera." He scuffed as he unlocked the last shackle on my wrist.

As soon as my hands were free, I started massaging my wrists. The pain from the restraints had left my wrists sore and tender.

"How do you know my name?" I asked curiously. "Do I know you?" I tried to focus on his voice to see if I recognized it. He stood there staring at me as I waited for his reply. My patience was growing thin. I had no idea what time it was or how long I had been shackled.

"There you go with them damn questions again. "He scolded, turning around to walk away. "Don't you know when to shut the hell up?" He continued.

This was my chance. I seized the opportunity, swiftly sliding forward and delivering a powerful kick behind his kneecap. The impact caused him to drop to his knees, completely caught off guard by the sudden attack. Before he could turn around or comprehend what had just happened, I swiftly followed up with a knee strike to the side of his head. The force of the blow was enough to send him crashing to the floor. With adrenaline coursing through my veins, I struggled to regain my balance, standing on shaky legs before him. His eyes remained open as he lay on the ground, seemingly in a daze.

It was a moment of hesitation as I stood in the makeshift prison, contemplating my next move. The decision weighed heavily on my mind. Should I continue my assault on him or make a desperate run for freedom? The adrenaline surged through my veins as I quickly turned, determined to make a dash for the door. But just as I began my escape, he reached out and grabbed hold of my foot, causing me to stumble and fall. The impact jolted through my body, momentarily disorienting me. I struggled to regain my balance, my heart pounding in my chest.

As I turned around, I saw him slowly rising to his feet. His eyes burned with hatred, reflecting the pain and anger that consumed him. Without a moment's hesitation, I lashed out, aiming a kick towards him. He was quick to defend himself, skillfully blocking my attack. His right arm swung across, narrowly missing my face. I quickly came back with two quick jabs to his head and a knee to his side, causing him to waver. I dropped to the floor, kicking his foot from under him. I stood up, prepared to deliver another blow once he fell.

As anticipated, he dropped to one knee but shot me an uppercut that sent my head flying back, causing me to stumble backward in a daze. I looked at him with double vision as he strolled towards me. I shook my head, trying to regain my composure. I grabbed the metal folding chair and swung it towards him. He grabbed the chair mid-swing, snatching it from me and tossing it to the other side of the room.

"Ugh!" he screamed as he forcefully lifted me and flung me against the wall.

A surge of pain rippled through my body as I slid to the floor. With a menacing stride, he advanced toward me and grabbed me by the neck. His fingernails dug into my flesh as he vigorously slammed me against the wall with one hand. The impact sent shockwaves through my body, leaving me disoriented and gasping for breath. I desperately struggled to loosen his hands from around my neck. My feet dangled in the air, unable to find solid ground.

"So, you want to do things the hard way!" he yelled, his words dripping with anger.

He slammed his fist into my face with each word, each hit landing a crushing blow. The pain intensified with each punch, blurring my vision and numbing my senses.

Finally, after what felt like an eternity, he released his grip on my neck, still delivering non-stop blows to my face. I collapsed to the floor, my body limp and battered. My hands instinctively moved to cover my face, shielding it from further harm. I unintentionally yanked off his mask while trying to defend myself from his relentless attacks. A gasp escaped my lips as I stared at his face, which I knew all too well.

"Brayden," I whispered in disbelief just before his fist came down on my face, causing darkness to surround me once again.

☐

CHAPTER 11

Brayden

"You dumb bitch!" I yelled as I pounded my fist into her face, knocking her ass out.

I stepped back, my chest heaved up and down as I tried to catch my breath. Her unconscious body was sprawled out on the floor, her face swollen and bloody. I felt a sense of satisfaction looking at her motionless body. My anger had indeed gotten the best of me. I figured Glen taught Ciera how to fight. I've never seen her spar with anyone but damn, I had to come with it. If I hadn't gotten the upper hand by throwing her ass against the wall, she might have knocked me out and fucked up my plans. I bent down, touching her neck to check for a pulse, and that's when I noticed my ski mask in her hand.

"Shit!" I yelled, kicking her in her stomach. This bitch was alive, and she saw my face. The last thing I wanted was for her to know who I was. "I should have known this bitch wouldn't listen." I fumed as I wiped the sweat dripping from my face.

I looked at the back of my hand, realizing it wasn't sweat but blood trickling down my face. I stared at my hand momentarily, thinking of a new plan. Turning my back towards Ciera, I paced the floor as it hit me. I grinned at the thought of Ciera unknowingly helping me to come up with an addition to my already perfect plan. What happens next will be her own damn fault.

I picked her up and tossed her on the mattress. I removed her hoodie to wipe the blood from her face that constantly dripped from the gashes on the side of her eyes and lips. I yanked her pants off and used it to soak up some of the blood that saturated the carpet. I went back to Ciera and chained up her wrists. I'll be damned if I let her ass up this time around. I thought as I shackled up her ankles.

I stood back, admiring her with only her green bra and panties on. Ciera had definitely gained some muscle since the last time we were involved. I couldn't stop the smile from forming as I took in her perky breasts and thin waist. Her flat stomach showed off her well-defined six-pack even in her unconscious state. I noticed how beautiful she had gotten since the last time I claimed her as mine.

I massaged my dick while I continued to marvel at her sexiness. My face twisted in a frown at the thought of Keon taking what should have belonged to me. I outta take that nigga's life too. I thought as I pulled my pants down.

"You may be his bitch, but until I decide to let you go, your ass is mine," I growled to Ciera while she lay unconscious as I pulled off her panties and took what I was entitled to.

After bagging Ciera's bloodied clothes and leaving her locked in her dark room, I headed upstairs. I fixed myself a couple of burgers, grabbed a beer from the fridge, and plopped my ass on my sofa. Turned on a basketball game and watched my man LeBron dominate the court as I enjoyed the rest of my evening.

As I ate and watched the game, I thought about the next phase of my plan. I figured it would be wise to lay low for a while, but first, I needed to make a call. I pulled out my phone and scrolled down to the number I needed. I dialed the number and waited for the other party to pick up. After a few rings, a voice answered.

"What's up, Bayden?" I smiled to myself.

"Hey Levi, I need a favor."

"Sure, it'll cost you though." He answered with confidence.

"No, it won't." I laughed. "You know how much dirt I got on you man? Let's not forget all the money I used to help you out of your sticky situations. I could easily turn everything over to the authorities if-"

"Alright, alright. What, you need a man?" He replied, sounding defeated.

"I need you to plant some items for me. Being a cop and all, this type of shit is right up your alley."

"Whatever." When do you need this done?" he murmured.

"Aw come on, Levi, where is that cocky-ass attitude you always have? We're partners," I teased, sipping my beer.

"Fuck you Brayden, we aren't partners! You're blackmailing a cop." He scowled.

Beer flew out my mouth as I tried to suppress my laughter. Levi was always stern and in control. To hear him flustered and angry was hilarious.

"Now you want to claim cop status after all the dirt you're wearing? Get the fuck outta here!" I laughed. "Listen, I need this done in two weeks tops. I want these people to sulk in their grief and worry before I give them the satisfaction of seeing what you'll be planting," I laughed.

"Yeah man, whatever just leave it at the spot along with the information. I'm not too fond of phones. This makes us even Brayden." He said. I could hear the confidence in his voice coming back.

"Says who? Certainly not you Levi." I laughed. "You're killing me with this conversation. I'll let you know when your debt is paid. Until then, be available if and when I need you again." I said before disconnecting the call.

He grumbled something unintelligible before the line went dead. Levi may be a cop, but this was my game we were playing, and I used my pawns as I saw fit.

☐

CHAPTER 12

Brielle

I shrieked as my eyes snapped open. I sat up in bed, drenched in sweat. My heart was pounding as I quickly looked around in a panic, realizing I was in my room. Just another nightmare, I thought to myself as I took a deep breath. It's been two weeks since I found out CeCe was missing, and it infuriates me to think that I had to find out my cousin was missing through Ami.

Ami is our boss from Ami's Boutique. She called to inform me that CeCe was an hour late for her shift and hadn't called in. I recalled the phone call that changed my life.

"Hey, Ami!" I greeted.

"How you doing Brielle? I was wondering, have you heard from Ciera?"

"No, not today. Why?"

"Oh. She was supposed to start her shift at four today. It's five o'clock, and she isn't here."

"Hmm… That's not like her."

"No, it's not. I've called her several times, no answer. If you get a hold of her, can you tell her she has an hour to get here before I write her up for no call, no show?"

"I'll try to track her down and pass on the message for you."

"Thanks, Brielle." She sighed before disconnecting the call.

I immediately called Ciera's cell twice, and it was sent to voicemail. I rang her home phone and got the same result. I racked my brain, trying to figure out where she would be. Knowing how much CeCe likes to work out, the gym popped into my mind, so I decided to try her there. I called Diamond Securities since that is the only gym she used.

"Good evening, you've reached Diamond Security. Kim speaking, how may I direct your call?"

"Hi, Kim. This is Brielle. Do you know if Ciera's in the office today?"

"No, I'm sorry she isn't."

"Are you sure she's not in the gym?"

"I'm positive. The gym is closed for cleaning as of right now. Besides, Ciera normally doesn't hit the gym on Mondays."

"Oh yeah, that's right, I forgot. Okay. Thanks Kim."

"No problem Brielle. See you soon." I heard before hanging up.

I sat back in my car, having just finished my last class. Alisha Keys' You Don't Know My Name flowed softly through the speakers as I made my calls. I wasn't sure about her class schedule since we had just started a new semester. For all I knew, she could be in class right now. Maybe she forgot to update Ami on her new class schedule.

I decided to dial Uncle Glen and pass the message on to him to give to CeCe. When he didn't answer, I immediately called Aunt Sherry. I started to get frustrated when she failed to answer her phone.

"What is going on with everyone today!" I yelled out in frustration.

I had better things to do than trying to find CeCe. I had an appointment for my dress fitting, and I already had homework to start. Lastly, I had to meet with Loyal to finalize the guest list.

I decided to make one last attempt. I figured I'd give Keon a call. If anyone knew where Ciera was, it would be him, and If he didn't answer, then CeCe would just have to take her write-up. By the fourth ring, just as I was about to hang up, he answered.

"Hello," he greeted, his voice thick with excitement.

I was so excited that I had gotten a hold of someone that I blurted out. "Finally! Do you have any idea where CeCe is?" I huffed with a little more attitude than I attended. I realized my mistake as soon as the words left my mouth. "I'm sorry, Keon. I'm not irritated with you. It's just that I've spent the last ten minutes trying to call her, and she's not answering. I can't even get in touch with her mom or dad. Please tell me you're with CeCe right now." There was a long pause. "Hello?" I spoke before I took the phone away from my ear to make sure the line wasn't disconnected.

"No," he answered dryly.

"Ugh!" I sighed. "I don't know what to do. Ami called. CeCe is late for work and will get a write-up if she's not there within the hour. Can you pass the message on to her when you can? It seems like you might have a better chance of getting in touch with her than me." There was another pregnant pause. "Hello... Keon?" I called out again before looking at the phone again. I jumped at a loud thud, followed by a shattering sound, coming through the phone.

"Have you talked to Glen or your dad?" he snapped.

"No… I mean, I called, but nobody is answering my calls. Is everything okay? Are you and CeCe still good?" I asked.

I started to get worried. I could tell something was wrong from the anger coming through the phone. I've never seen Keon upset before, and now that he's bringing up my dad and uncle, those words sent shivers down my spine.

"No, everything is not okay." He yelled. "Ciera's been kidnapped. You should call your dad. I have to go." He said before disconnecting the call.

I froze, holding the phone to my ears as his last statement played repeatedly in my head. The news hit me like a ton of bricks, and since then, I've been consumed by worry and fear.

I jumped, startled at my dad, throwing my bedroom door open. He had a black towel tied around his waist and a worried look on his face.

"Is everything okay?" he asked, breathless as he looked around the room. My mom poked her head inside the room from behind my dad.

"Yeah, I'm sorry. I had another nightmare," I exhaled.

"Awe, baby," my mom cried as she rushed to my bed to comfort me in a hug. She wore a red turtleneck sweater dress, black leggings, and black boots. She looked over at my dad. "It's okay babe, I got her. Go finish getting dressed." He gave her a nod and walked out of the room. My mom sat on my bed. I slid down and put my head in her lap. "Who was it about this time, you or Ciara?" she asked as she played in my hair.

"Me… I was locked in a dark room." I sobbed. I was cold and in so much pain." I waited for her to reply, but instead, she remained quiet and continued playing in my hair. "I hate this mama.

Since CeCe's been missing, I've been having these nightmares every night, it seems."

"Have you ever been able to see anything… other than a dark room?" she asked.

"No"

"What about a person? Have you seen anyone in your dream?"

"No, why?" I asked, baffled.

"You and CeCe were always close. Growing up, you two were more like siblings than cousins. From the moment you heard that she had gone missing, you've felt like a part of you is missing, don't you?"

I sat up on the bed, finally looking at her. "Well, yeah! Don't you?" I asked. "She's your niece."

"Yeah, I do." She replied, nodding her head. "What I meant is that you're so close to Ciera. Basically, what I'm getting at is, what if these nightmares you're having are really Ciera's reality that you're seeing?"

I shook my head. "That's impossible," I replied, lying back down on her lap. She was quiet in deep thought, obviously trying to think of a way to prove her point. I closed my eyes, listening to the sound of her fingers combing through my hair. I could feel myself relaxing.

"Maybe not. Do you remember your eighteenth birthday?"

I rolled my eyes, wondering what this had to do with my nightmares or Ciera. "Of course, I do, Mama, but what does this have to do with Ciera?" I asked, trying not to show my frustration.

"Just answer the question." she urged.

A sigh escaped my lips as I answered her. "Uncle Glen, Aunt Sherry, and CeCe came over. We did the cake and gift thing, then danced, ate, and said our goodbyes."

"Are you sure?"

"Ugh… Mama, I don't under-"

"I remember that"." she said, cutting me off, "but I also remember that day being the worst day of our lives. Think Brielle." She pushed.

"Mama, you're confusing me. I don't know what you're talking about." Her eyes filled with tears as she laid my head back on her lap and started playing with my hair again.

"I remember being depressed. I also remember being a flight attendant," she said in a broken voice. She sighed deeply as if the pain of those memories were still fresh. "I remember a terrible accident and us grieving the loss of your dad." She sobbed.

I was at a loss for words once realization sat in. "I- I thought that was a dream."

"No baby… That's what actually happened on your birthday."

My heart sank as my mind replayed all those events from that year. I thought back to how empty my life was without my dad. I remembered the feeling of loneliness and sadness that haunted me then. Grandma Kitty flashed in my mind, reminding me of the times I went into the past. "I thought that was a nightmare," I confessed as silent tears slid from my eyes. My heart ached at the thought of losing my dad again.

"How was I even able to go into the past? And how is it that you remember?" I asked.

She gave me a little smirk. "I believe it comes from my side of the family. Growing up, I heard stories of a few women in our family being able to go back in time but never about them changing reality. It's said that this ability jumps around from generation to generation.

As she told her story, I leaned back against the headboard and gave her my full attention. She leaned back, resting her head against the headboard, but her eyes were focused as if she were daydreaming. "Why is this the first time I've heard about this?" I questioned.

She shrugged her shoulders. "I thought it was an old folktale... until it happened to me."

"Mom!" I gasped.

I tried to keep my anger at bay. She felt the need to open up for some reason, and I didn't want to ruin the moment. I bit down on my tongue to stop myself from speaking, but the words still came out through clenched teeth.

"You gave me a hard time when I told you what was happening to me. You tried to make me think I was crazy. If you knew what was happening, why didn't you tell me or better yet, help me?'

Her gaze dropped to her lap as she picked at her leggings. "I guess I was in denial. I didn't want you to go through that again. I didn't know how to help you." She admitted.

"So, what is this... a family curse?"

I used to think so until you brought your father back." She smiled.

"Do you think he remembers? Do you think anyone remembers?"

She shook her head. "No, I questioned him as well as Sherry and Glen, about your eighteenth birthday. They only remember the altered version."

"And I'm guessing you and I," I said, pointing to myself and her, "only remember because we're... gifted?

"Yep, it would seem so," she replied.

"Ugh, being able to remember things others can't is a burden. It makes it hard to distinguish between what really happened and what didn't. I can't believe this whole time. I thought It was a dream."

We stayed silent for a while, each lost in our own thoughts. This was a lot to process, but I still had questions. I glanced at her, fixing myself to ask another question, but the look on her face told me she was fighting her own battles mentally. She looked sad and on the verge of tears but then blinked them away.

"It's been a year since daddy's been back. Why tell me this now?"

"Well, as you know, they are having a hard time finding Ciera. That's mainly because they don't have enough information to go on..."

"And you want me to go back to the day she was taken to see if I could come up with more information?" I gave a sideways smirk as I finished her sentence.

An uncertain look crossed her face as she shrugged her shoulders. "Maybe"

"Mom!" I sighed. "As much as I would love to help find CeCe anyway I can... What you're asking me to do is impossible."

"How is it impossible? You did it before, several times."

"Yeah, a year or so ago. Up until a moment ago, I thought it was a dream. I don't even know how I did it." I added. I was done with this conversation. I slid out of the bed and paced the floor. It was so selfish of her to ask this of me. If she had known about this so-called gift all this time, why didn't she go into the past herself? I fumed to myself.

My mom stared at me briefly before rushing over to embrace me. I didn't realize I was sobbing until she held me against her chest. "I'm sorry for stressing you out more than you already are. I thought this might help. Don't worry, Brie, we'll think of something else. We'll find another way to bring Ciera home." She whispered while holding me.

A knock at the door startled both of us. Daddy peaked his head in the room. "You ladies done in here? If so, I'm ready Brenda... we need to be heading out."

"Wait... you guys are leaving? Where are you going?" I asked.

"We're meeting up with Glen and Sherry." He answered, stepping further into my room. He was wearing grey sweatpants, a white T-shirt and white tennis.

"Wait, let me get dressed. I'll come with you. It won't take-"

"I thought you had plans with Loyal today?" he asked, cutting me off.

"Yeah, Brie, didn't you say you had a meeting with the caterers today?" She asked, finally letting go of our embrace to look at me.

"Yeah, but... wait a minute. Ya'll really expect me to continue planning a wedding while Ciera is missing? Ah... no, that's not happening." I fumed. My cheeks were covered in hot tears as I searched my closet for an outfit. "The wedding is canceled! How can you guys even think I would plan this wedding without her?" I sobbed as I yanked every piece of clothing off my hangers. "She's my maid of honor!" I screamed as my dad ran to me, catching me before I fell to the floor. "I can't do this without her." I cried in his arms as he squeezed me tightly.

My mother caressed my head. "No Brie." She whispered as she cried.

"Shhh." My dad whispered to me as he rocked me in his arms.

"Listen to me, Brielle! We are not going to break down like this… you understand me?" he asked as he squeezed my head between his palms, forcing me to look at him. "We're going to find Ciera, and because of that, you're going to continue planning the wedding so that she has something to look forward to when she returns. Do you hear me?" He asked. "I know things look bad right now, but you need to have faith."

"How can I when they don't have any leads? If they did, they would have found her already!" I screamed.

"Brielle!" he yelled as he applied pressure to the sides of my head. "Because if you don't have faith, you have nothing. Without faith, there is no hope. Now get dressed. I'll call Loyal and ask him to reschedule the meeting. I'll be in the living room." He said as he helped me up. My mom kissed my forehead before following him out the door.

"Mama," I called out, trying to calm myself down. She turned around with one hand still on the doorknob. You mentioned that this happened to you. What happened that made you never want to revisit the past?"

"Brielle… I really don't want to-"

"Mom, please, I need to know?" I asked, interrupting her.

She sighed, taking her eyes off me and focusing on the wall behind me as if a movie was projected onto the wall. "I got stuck watching my older sister, who I didn't know I had, get murdered by her stepmother.

"Huh," I gasped, covering my mouth. "Mom... but wait, how did you know she was your sister?"

"Your grandmother walked into the house with me on her hip right after she was murdered. I was too young to remember." She wiped tears from her cheek.

"Oh Mama, I'm so sorry. I didn't even know you had a sister."

"I didn't either. That's how your grandmother wanted it. I guess it was easier for her not to talk about her. If it wasn't for me going to the past, I would have never even known her name."

"What was her name?"

She stared at me with a small smile. "Gabrielle." She said, her voice cracking. She stood silent for a moment, remembering the sister she never got a chance to know. "Hurry up and get dressed. We need to get going," she said as she wiped her tears and walked out the door.

I quickly dressed. My heart heavy with sadness. But happy to know I was named after the aunt I never knew I had. I was stunned by the new information. In all my life, I had never heard my mother speak of her sister before. I knew there was a lot I didn't know about my family's history on my mother's side, but I never expected this.

My ten o'clock alarm went off on my phone. I moaned as I cut it off. The day had just started, and I was already emotionally drained. I quickly ran to the bathroom to freshen up. I trotted back to my room, slipped on some gray acid-wash jeans and a black shirt, and stuffed my foot into my black high-top sneakers. I grabbed my purse and walked out of my room.

When I rounded the corner, I saw my dad dive onto my mom and scream, "Get down!"

☐

CHAPTER 13

Brielle

The rapid Rat-Tat-Tat-Tat sound of gunfire echoed through the air, piercing the moment's stillness. It was accompanied by the urgent shout of my father, "Brielle, get the fuck down!" Those words snapped me back into reality. At that moment, I berated myself internally for freezing, knowing full well the protocols of a shootout. My father had ingrained them into me. Hell, I even owned a gun myself.

Growing up, my father always stressed the importance of being prepared for dangerous situations. He had drilled it into me, teaching me the necessary skills to survive a shootout. This, being my first encounter with such a terrifying event, was no excuse. I shouldn't have allowed myself to freeze, and I just knew my father would chew me out for this.

I dropped to the floor in a panic, now only worrying about the safety of my parents. The thought of being parentless squeezed my heart. After talking with my mom, I remembered that pain all too well. Even though it was short-lived, I didn't want to go through that again.

As the echoes of gunfire continued to ring in my ear, I shifted my head in search of my parents. I was still in the hallway. I could partially see them on the living room floor from where I was. Their heads were near the front door. My dad was still on top of my mother, protecting her with his body. He shifted his head back in my direction.

"Stay right there, Brielle!" he shouted, just enough for me to hear him. It was as if he knew I was about to belly crawl down the hallway towards them.

Shots rang out as I lay my head on the floor. I shut my eyes tightly, praying the chaos would soon be over. There had to be at least two shooters. I knew shots were coming from the front of the house, but I also saw bullets flying in from the side of the house near my parents' room.

"aaargh, shit!" my dad screamed out.

Just before the shooting stopped, I heard a loud crash through my parents' bedroom window. I didn't want to be lying on the hallway floor if someone came through the window, so I quickly crawled over to my parents and lay down on the floor next to them. After what felt like an eternity, a heavy silence filled the house.

"Mom, Dad... are you okay?"

"Shhh. Brie, stay down and keep quiet," he whispered through gritted teeth as he pushed my head back down to the floor.

My anger spiked at him, forcing my head down like I was a child. It took everything in me not to snap back. We heard two car doors slam and tires screeching as a car sped away.

"Stay here," My dad whispered as he got up and crept to the living room wall. He pressed his back against the wall and peeked out the shattered window. Do not move, he muttered as he walked around us to check the rest of the house. I could hear the pieces of glass shattering under his footsteps. My heart raced as I heard more glass breaking from the back of the house.

We waited in silence until he came back. "All clear, I just called the cops. Ya'll okay?" he asked, coming out of the hallway. I got up and dusted pieces of glass off me while he rushed over to help my mother off the floor.

"Ugh," she moaned as she rubbed the back of her head. "My head hurts. I hit the floor hard from you diving on me."

"I'm sorry, babe," he said, kissing her forehead. "I only had a split second to think when I saw them lift their guns up." He turned his gaze to me, caressing my shoulder. "What about you? Are you hurt?"

"No, I don't think so," I replied while patting myself down.

"Good. Now, what the hell were you thinking freezing up like that? You could have been killed!" he snapped.

I rolled my eyes. I knew it was coming. "Daddy," I sighed, "I just-"

"Don't daddy me! We went over this a thousand times."

"Gerald, can't this wait?" My mom pleaded with him, trying to come to my rescue.

"Hell no! Who's to say they won't be back? What the fuck am I training her for if it goes in one ear and out the-"

"Dad!" I screamed out, "Are you kidding me right now?" I made one mistake. A big mistake. I get it! I've already beat myself up about it, and I don't need you trying to make me feel worse than I already do. And stop treating me like a child. I'm not fourteen years old anymore"!" I shouted as I picked my purse off the floor and took out my cell phone to call Loyal.

"Who the hell do you think you're talking to?" He shouted as he made his way towards me. "I don't care how old you are, don't you ever-"

"Would you two stop it!" my mom shouted, interrupting my dad. She stepped in front of him, placed her hands on his chest, and pushed him back.

"I'm not about to let her-"

"Gerald, please!" my mother said in a tone that said don't try me.

"Now, we all have had a very trying morning. I know emotions are high right now, but that does not give you two the right to blow up on each other. It's a blessing that we're even breathing right now. Did you even take the chance to look around you? Look at this house!" she yelled.

I sighed, knowing my mom was right. Just a minute ago, I was worried about losing one of them. I knew my dad was overprotective. He's been like that my whole life. It took me a moment to take in my surroundings. My dad's navy blue reclining chair sat in the corner. Bullet holes and cotton came through the fabric. The same went for the gray sectional chase that sat across from the chair. The small white side table on the side of my dad's chair was fine, but the silver lamp on top was busted. Our flat-screen TV was shot up. The walls were riddled with bullet holes of different sizes around the house. The kitchen cabinets and the dining room were also a mess. Everything was a mess, and I hadn't seen the bedrooms yet.

"My mom was right. It was a blessing we were alive. I kicked myself mentally again for letting my emotions get the best of me. "Mama's right. I'm sorry, Daddy." I apologized. "Are you okay?"

He turned away from me, pulled out his phone, and went to take a seat on his recliner. "I'm alright. I got grazed on my shoulder, but I'm good." He said while he perused his cell phone.

"What!" My mom drew in a breath.

"Oh my God! Daddy!" I said.

"Why didn't you say something?" My mom yelled as we both rushed towards the side of him, looking at his shoulders.

He had a rip in his shirt sleeve and small amounts of blood over his left shoulder. I mentally prepared myself as I lifted his sleeve and discovered two parallel abrasions. A small patch of spared skin separated the two wounds. The edges of the skin surrounding the wound looked as though it was singed. The sight of it gave me creeps. However, I couldn't help but be thankful that he only suffered a minor wound. The thought of how close he came to losing his life again left me speechless. I slowly backed away from him and sat on the sofa as if in a trance.

"Babe, it's most certainly a graze, and it looks disgusting!" She squirmed at the sight of it. "I can't believe you're so calm. It doesn't hurt?" My mom asked, still looking at his wound.

"Yeah, shit burns like hell, but I'll be alright." He replied, pulling his shirt down over his shoulder.

"Yo," Uncle Glen's voice came through the speakerphone. "Yawl on the way?"

"Naw man. We were ambushed. Some fools shot up the house."

"Come again!" Uncle Glen replied.

"You heard right. Luckily, I saw them fools when I did. We were just about to step out," My dad grabbed my mom's hand from his shoulder and swung her around to sit on his lap.

"Anyone hurt?"

"Everyone is fine. I got grazed, but I'm good."

"We'll be there in fifteen," Uncle Glen said before disconnecting the call.

Time seemed to stand still with everyone quiet, lost in their own thoughts. I got up and headed towards the kitchen. "You want me to get you something to drink?" I asked, looking back and forth between the both of them. They both shook their heads.

"No," My mom answered barely above a whisper.

Her response shocked me. I was ready to break open one of her wine bottles. When she's stressed, she usually craves wine the most. I rummaged through the cabinets, trying to find a glass that wasn't broken. Once I found one, I washed it and went to the fridge. I stood in front of the open fridge for a moment. To my parents, it probably looked like I was trying to decide what to drink when I was actually thinking about how today could have turned disastrous and gruesome. The last thing I ever wanted to do again was see my parents' bloodied bodies. I was not in the mood to grieve the loss of another parent. The vibration of my phone snapped me out of my thoughts. It was a text from Loyal.

LOYAL: Hey, Brie. Just wanted to let you know I rescheduled the meeting with Linda for Saturday at twelve noon. Let me know if that date and time doesn't work for you.

I called him back while grabbing the milk carton from the fridge. Thankfully, it was the only beverage not riddled with bullet holes. I set the carton on the counter and bent down to grab the protein shake mix from the bottom cabinet. I held the phone to my ear with my shoulder as I started to make my shake.

"Hello my queen. Did you get my text?"

I took a deep breath and closed my eyes. Letting his deep voice calm my nerves. His voice had a calming effect on me, and I felt some of my anxiety melt away. "Yes, I did. Thank you."

"What happened to you this morning?" he asked.

"I had an emotional breakdown. I'm worried about my cousin, and I had another nightmare." I sighed. "It's just been a crazy morning. I had a heart-to-heart with my mom and discovered some family secrets or drama. Whatever you want to call it." I spoke softly, not wanting my parents to hear my conversation.

"Well…" His voice strained while he stretched. "You know I'm here for you if you want to talk about it."

I'm still undecided on telling Loyal about me going back into the past. Up until now, I thought it was nothing more than a dream. Having learned it's hereditary, I may have to tell him if we have a daughter, but then again, my father doesn't even know. How would a person even act when hearing something like this? Nothing about this is normal. I took a sip of my vanilla smoothie, figuring I'd just decided to keep him in the dark.

"What do you have planned for the day."

"Nothing, since I had to cancel our plans. You?"

"I umm… I was heading out with my parents, but… something… happened."

I bit down on my bottom lip. I felt nervous telling him about the shooting. Loyal could be just as overprotective as my dad. Even though I loved Loyal, we held no secrets from each other. I felt there was another side to him. He didn't have anger issues or anything. He never put his hands on me. It was a vibe that I sometimes got from Loyal, his brother Trust, and his dad.

"What happened?" He asked, his voice taking a more serious tone.

I took another sip of my shake and turned around, leaning against the counter. I looked at my parents, still sitting in the same spot. Then, I glanced at all the damage done around the house.

"Brielle! What happened?"

"Listen, Loyal... before your adrenalin kicks in, just know I'm fine. My parents are okay."

"Woman! If you don't stop beating around the bush."

"Alright, alright already... the house was shot up this morning." There was a brief moment of silence before he calmly answered.

"And you're okay?"

"Yes"

"And no one was hurt?"

"No, I mean... well, my dad got grazed, but he says he's okay."

"You should have mentioned this the moment I answered your call. "I'm on my way." I heard the jingle of his keys and the door slam just before the line disconnected.

Uncle Glen and Aunt Sherry were the first to arrive. My dad got up to open the door before he could ring the bell. My dad and uncle exchanged hugs without saying a word. The scowl on his face and his body language said enough. Aunt Sherry walked in behind Uncle Glen.

"Gerald!" She whined with open arms, ready to embrace him. There was a duffle bag hanging over her shoulder. I knew it was her medical bag. She was an RN, but if you didn't know her, you would swear she was a doctor. She was always ready to help someone in need. She hugged my dad and kissed his cheek.

"I'm good, Sherry. Don't worry yourself." My dad said while he closed the door behind her.

"That's impossible. That seems to be the only thing I know how to do these days." She said as she made her way to the living room in search of my mom and me. She let her duffle bag drop from her shoulder onto the floor beside the sofa. "How can I not worry?" She cried as she ran to my mom and embraced her.

I sat my shake down and walked over to greet my aunt. She quickly pulled me in on the embrace and tightly squeezed my mom and me while she cried.

"Hey Aunt Sherry"

"Hi, girl. We're alright." My mom said, caressing her back.

"Are you sure?" Aunt Sherry asked.

"Yeah, we're just a little shaken up." My mom answered, breaking our embrace.

"What the hell is going on around here?" Aunt Sherry huffed, taking a seat on the couch.

"That's what I want to know." Uncle Glen responded.

He stood in the center of the room, taking in all the damage. His arms were folded across his chest. My dad sat in his chair with his elbow propped on his knees while he massaged his temples. Aunt Sherry grabbed her duffle bag and approached my dad, preparing to care for his wound.

"Did you call the cops?" Uncle Glen asked.

"Yeah, they should be here any minute." My dad responded.

"How many shooters?"

"Three."

"Did you get a good look at them?"

"Naw, they wore scream masks with some dumb-looking top hats."

Uncle Glen finally took a seat on the couch. "Damn. Do you think there's a connection? What are the odds of Ciera getting kidnapped and then this happening." He said, gesturing to the bullet hole-stained walls.

Daddy sighed. "Glen, I was just thinking that. And if there is a connection..."

"There you go!" Aunt Sherry said, patting his arm. "All cleaned and bandaged up. That should hold you."

"Thanks, Sherry." My dad said as she put away her supplies.

I was startled by three hard knocks at the door, "Police!" A deep feminine voice yelled from behind the door.

"I'll get it!" I shouted as I rushed to the door, trying to play it off that the knock made me jump. We just had a life-or-death situation, and nobody seemed startled but me. I snatched the door open to find a tall, brawny woman. She was heavily built and had a brick wall-type figure. Her black, wavy hair was swept into a tight low bun. Her skin was a medium sandy beige, and she had blue eyes.

"There were reports of a shooting?" she asked.

"Yes, officer, please come in." I stepped to the side and opened the door wider for her. I didn't notice the officer behind her until he walked inside.

"Good afternoon. My name is Officer Romo, and this is my partner, Officer Levi." She said as she walked in and nodded towards the officer behind her.

"No, the fuck he ain't! Is this a joke?" laughed Uncle Glen, looking at my dad.

"Excuse me?" Officer Romo asked, confused.

"Levi is not welcome in this house." Uncle Glen said with a more serious tone.

"Officer Levi" he corrected.

"Naw buddy, you that title when you disrespected me in my office." Uncle Glen stated.

Levi put up both hands to surrender. I thought that strange coming from a cop. It was clear that this man must have come across my uncle wrong.

"Mr. Taylor" Levi said looking between both Uncle Glen, and my dad, "I'm just here to help. Officer Romo is my temporary partner. We were the only ones close to the area when the call came in."

I had no idea what was going on but the tension in the room was suffocating.

Aunt Sherry walked to Uncle Glen, caressing his back. "It's okay, Glen, just let them do their job." She sighed.

"Whatever, man!" Uncle Glen said, breaking away from her touch and taking a seat on the couch.

"Thank you," Levi grinned at Aunt Sherry.

"I didn't do this for you. I just want to hurry up and get this day over." She snapped.

"Understood," Levi stated, with a nod of his head.

"Was anyone hurt?" Officer Romo asked again.

"No," my dad stated. "I got grazed, but I'm alright." He said.

"Is this your resident or his?" she asked, pointing to Uncle Glen.

"It's mine. I live here with my wife and daughter." He pointed at my mother and me.

"Are you sure you don't want medical treatment?" Levi asked.

My dad cut his eyes at him, giving him a silent stare before answering, "No. As I said... I'm alright."

"Did you see the shooter?" Officer Romo asked.

"Yeah." My dad sighed. "There were three of them. They had on scream masks and some funky ass-looking top hats."

"Do you know anyone who would want to harm you or your family? Any enemies?" Levi asked.

"You mean besides you?" Uncle Glen exclaimed from his seat.

"Glen, seriously!" Sherry shouted.

"No, not that we're aware of," Dad stated.

Officer Romo looked around before asking, "Do you mind if we look around at all the damage?"

"No, go ahead." My mom answered.

"Thank you, ma'am." Officer Romo said before she and Officer Levi made their way down the hall.

Ding-Dong, "I'll get it! It's Loyal." I blurted out as I jogged to the door. Loyal scooped me up and spun me around.

"Oh my god, woman! Are you sure you're okay?" he asked while gently placing my feet back on the floor. He gave me a peck on the lips.

"Yeah, I'm fine."

"What about you all?" Everyone okay?" he asked, walking to the living room with my hand in his.

"Hey, Loyal" Aunt Sherry greeted, rubbing her temples.

"What's up, son." My dad sighed.

"Yo" Uncle Glen, gave Loyal a nod.

"Hey, sweetheart," My mom reached out embracing Loyal in a hug.

"Ya'll alright?" Loyal asked again.

"Yeah, we good. My dad responded.

Officer Romo returned to the living room. "That's a significant amount of damage. I highly recommend you stay elsewhere until your home or at least your windows have been replaced."

Loyal elbowed me softly in my side. "You're staying with me." He whispered in my ear. "I know your pops gone trip, but I'm not taking no for an answer."

I shrugged my shoulders in response. I had a feeling they would stay with Uncle Glen and Aunt Sherry, and I honestly didn't want to step foot in that house until Ciera returned. I continued to watch the exchange between my parents and Officer Romo. I realized Officer Levi was missing just as he walked out of the hallway.

"Gerald, you said nobody here was hurt… but this is a lot of blood for someone that's not hurt. Don't you think?" he said, holding up a white hoodie and blue jeans. My mom gasped.

"What the hell," my dad said. "Brielle… is that yours?"

I shook my head no. "That's my school's hoodie, but I have a black one."

"Nooo!" Aunt Sherry shrieked. She sobbed uncontrollably as she slowly walked to Officer Levi, grabbing the clothing from his hand. "That's Ciera's… That's what she was wearing the day she went missing. My baby!" she screamed as she dropped to the floor.

Uncle Glen immediately ran to her, lifting her off the floor. "What the hell! Where did you get that from?" he asked Levi.

"I found it under the desk in the office."

Uncle Glen turned his gaze to my dad. The raging look on his face had me holding my breath. He continued to console Aunt Sherry, who was still bawling her eyes out. She continued screaming out, "My baby!"

I didn't realize I was crying until I felt the drops on the back of my hand. I looked down, noticing for the first time that Loyal's arms were wrapped tightly around my waist, comforting me. The nightmare flashed in my mind and had me wondering if the person I saw was Ciera. She was obviously in pain or dead with the amount of blood covering her clothes.

My dad stood up angrily, ready to charge at Officer Levi. My mom held him back as she cried quietly. Officer Romo had her hand on her holster, ready to pull out her gun.

"What the hell Levi!" you planted that shit!" my dad roared.

"Why would I-"

"I don't even want to hear your wack-ass excuses. Don't think we didn't notice your ass back there longer than you should have been. This house ain't that fuckin big."

"Officer Romo, did you see that clothing anywhere in the office when you looked around?" my mom asked.

"I can't say that I did."

"Because that shit was planted!" my dad yelled.

"I had nothing in my hands when I did my search. I mean, come on, I walked in the house empty-handed." Officer Levi said in defense.

"That doesn't mean shit! Uncle Glen sneered.

Officer Levi shook his head as he walked towards the front door, making a call, "Detective…" I heard him say as he walked out of the house.

"Is this regarding a missing person case?" Officer Romo asked.

"Yes… my daughter was kidnapped two weeks ago." Uncle Glen responded.

Officer Romo shook her head in understanding. "In that case, you'll have to give your DNA sample. They will test the blood to see if it's a match to your daughters."

"Are you saying it might not be Ciera's blood?" Aunty Sherry asked.

Officer Romo shrugged her shoulders, "It's a possibility," she answered, not wanting to kill her hopes.

The officers left us in silence except for the occasional sniffing from the faces with the crying eyes. Me included. I wasn't expecting this turn of events. I couldn't get over the amount of blood that was soaked into those clothes.

"Glen, Sherry... I didn't take Ciera, and I damn sure didn't hurt my niece." It broke my heart to see my dad cry. Out of my twenty-three years of living, I have never seen a tear fall from his eyes. "That's my God-baby man! I would never...." Uncle Glen cut my dad off, rushing to embrace him in a tight, brotherly hug.

"I know man. I'm sorry." Uncle Glen cried as he patted my dad on the back twice. "Listen." He said as he let my dad go from their embrace. "How about yawl stay with Sherry and me until things get fixed around here." He said, gesturing to the damage inside the house.

"That sounds like a good idea." My mom stated.

"Brielle will be staying with me," Loyal said. My dad's jaw locked as his eyebrows furrowed together. I knew he was about to protest.

"Daddy, I can't stay there." I turned to Uncle Glen and Aunt Sherry. "I'm so sorry, but I can't go to that house until Ciera returns. I already know my parents are taking your guest bedroom, and I refuse to stay in Ciera's room." I cried.

"I understand." My mom said.

"Me too baby." Aunt Sherry agreed.

"I don't like this." My dad spoke.

"Gerald, Brielle is twenty-three years old, and he's her fiancé."

"Thank you, mama," I said to her, being on my side.

"Don't pop up here pregnant." My dad warned. "Not until after you say I do."

"I know daddy." I moaned as I got up to pack my bag. At that point, I was looking for any reason to be in a different room. My mom got up behind me.

"I'll go pack us a bag too." She said to my dad, giving him a peck on the cheek before walking away.

By the time we were packed and ready to go, Uncle Glen and my dad had all the busted windows boarded up with either cardboard or plywood, whichever was found in the garage. Loyal grabbed my bag off my shoulder.

"You ready?" he asked.

"Yeah... just let me say my goodbyes."

"Actually," My dad said. "We're all going to head down to the precinct to give up your precious DNA. I have a feeling they will end up requesting it from all of us anyway."

□

CHAPTER 14

Glen

"Glen… Glen!" Sherry said, shaking me awake.

I groaned before turning away from her. "Yeah," I answered, still half asleep.

"Your phone is vibrating." She said with a yawn.

I reached over and grabbed my phone from the nightstand, realizing it was Mike calling. "Hello," I answered in a raspy voice.

"Hey man, you still asleep?" Mike asked.

Not anymore. What's up?" I replied, my voice strained from stretching.

"I just wanted to let you know I'm in the office today."

"Alright, thanks for the update," I said, trying to shake off the grogginess. "Anything urgent?"

"Nah, nothing urgent." I heard what happened yesterday morning. Just wanted to sync up and see if you or Gerald needed anything."

I frowned. "You heard? How did you hear about it?" I quizzed.

"It's a few rumors floating around here. Levi's dumb ass came up here talkin' about Gerald's house being shot up yesterday morning."

"That dumb fuck. I don't know how much more of him I can take.

"I figured I'd reach out, ya'll good?"

"Physically, yeah. Mentally we lost as fuck."

"Bet. How about you and Gerald take the day off, have some family time, or whatnot. I'll hold it down here."

"Ay, I really appreciate you man." I said, sitting up on the edge of the bed."

"No problem. Before I let you go, Brayden is here. Did you have a meeting with him or something?"

With all the issues going on, I had to think about it. This wouldn't be the first time I've been forgetful regarding scheduled meetings. "Ah… not that I'm aware of. Why?" I asked, swinging my legs over the bed and sitting up.

"Dude, keep creeping past your office. I accessed his file, and his assignment ended two weeks ago. He didn't hit you up about reassignment?"

I let my head hang back and looked at the ceiling as I picked my brain. "Not that I can remember. When did you say his assignment ended?"

"Two weeks ago."

"That's about the same time Ciera went missing. Yo, honestly, I don't even know, man… my head has been-"

Mike interrupted me. "Aye, don't even explain yourself. I already know. I'll take care of that fool. Don't worry about it. I'll hit you up later."

As I hung up, a wave of appreciation washed over me. I couldn't help but feel a sense of gratitude for having a colleague like Mike. Amidst the chaos of the business world, he was one of the few individuals besides Gerald that I trusted wholeheartedly. Mike had been an integral part of our journey right from the beginning. When Gerald and I laid the foundation of our business, he was among the first individuals we brought on board. However, our connection with him extended far beyond our professional lives.

We had known Mike since our early college days, forging a bond that withstood the test of time. Unlike many of us, Mike was an only child and didn't have a family of his own. He dedicated his life to his work, becoming married to his job. On the day Ciera went missing, Gerald and I had just promoted him to manager director and given him his own office.

"What was that about?" Sherry asked, coming out of the bathroom and tying her black satin robe. Her hair was in a low ponytail. She walked over to me and gave me a quick peck on the lips, leaving a taste of mint on my lip. The smell of Listerine was strong on her breath.

"That was Mike. He offered to take care of things at the office today."

"That was nice of him." She said as she walked to the side of her dresser and slipped on her gray slippers. "I'm going to head down and start breakfast."

"Alright, babe, I'm going to freshen up before I head down," I said as I stood up. I smacked her on the ass when she passed me by. She turned to look at me, giving me a weak smile, before heading downstairs to the kitchen.

Nothing has been right since Ciera was taken. The house seems dead without my baby girl's sassiness. I find myself going to her room every night to feel close to her. It hurts how much I miss my daughter. I never in a million years thought something like this would happen to me or my family. It feels like a piece of my soul is missing. Though I try to stay strong, the thought of her out somewhere scared, alone, and possibly hurt breaks my heart.

After brushing my teeth and washing my face, I quickly threw on black and white plaid lounge pants and a white T-shirt. I stepped into my black house shoes and hurried out the door to help Sherry in the kitchen.

Forty minutes later, Gerald, Brenda, Sherry, and I sit at the dining table in our eat-in kitchen. Sherry cooked up a delicious breakfast. Egg scramble with bacon, cheese, and onions. Her famous banana-nut pancakes and hash browns. I came down to help her, but she only allowed me to make the coffee. She claimed cooking was her stress reliever.

Everyone ate in silence, each lost in their own thoughts. All that could be heard was the sound of forks scraping the plates and occasional chewing.

"Sherry, these pancakes are delicious," Brenda said before stuffing her mouth more.

"Thank you. These are Ciera's favorites." She reached over her plate to grab her coffee mug. "I made these for her the day she went missing." She took a sip and sat the mug down carefully while still looking down at the plate she'd barely eaten from. Silent tears fell from her eyes.

I noticed the deep, dark bags under Sherry's beautiful eyes for the first time in two weeks. Her eyes stayed swollen and red from all the crying she secretly does daily. Like me, she visits Ciera's room daily but waits until after she thinks I'm asleep. She's fighting to be strong but doesn't have to with me. I grab her hand off the table, lift it to my lips, and softly kiss the back of her hand.

"We'll get her back, babe," I tell her.

"Have you guys spoken to Keon lately?" Brenda asked, breaking the silence again.

"Yeah... he calls daily, hoping for an update."

"Yeah, and he stops by the house periodically to see if we're okay," I said, adding to Sherry's statement.

"You plan on telling him about the clothes that were found?" Gerald asked.

"I don't know Brah..."

"What's not to know?" Brenda said. "As much as we have grown to love and care for him, Keon is a grown-ass man." She said as she got up to wash her empty dish. "Don't hide this information from him. This is the reality we're dealt with, and if he chooses to go through it with us, then he can face this head-on with the rest of us." She said as she dried her dish and put it in the cabinet. She walked back to the table and took her seat next to Gerald.

"She has a point," Sherry said, nodding her head in agreement with Brenda.

Gerald sighed, placing both elbows on the table and massaging his temples. "I don't get it!" he shouted in frustration. "They take Ciera, hurt her, and plant the evidence on me. Why?"

"We don't know if it's Ciera's blood, Gerald. It could be anyone's," Sherry said in a hopeful tone.

"You're right, babe," I said, taking Sherry's hand. "And I hope it's not, but..." I turned my gaze back to Gerald." I'm not holding my breath. This was a well-thought-out plan. They knew shooting up the house would get the police involved and that they would find those clothes."

"Or plant it," Gerald said, staring at the floral centerpiece on the table. I could see his mind working, trying to put the puzzle together. However, there were too many missing pieces. "But why would the police plant it? We don't have no quarrel with them."

"Levi," I said, trying to help put the pieces together. "I have a problem with Levi… and he was the one that found it. He could have planted it."

"But your issue with Levi started the day Ciera went missing," Sherry said.

Gerald shook his head. "Yeah, this is too personal. I don't think it was Levi. Whoever this is trying to break up our family. A vendetta of some sort. If Levi was behind this, I think this would be a ransom issue."

"I still think one of the shooters planted it. It sounded like someone was in the house when Brielle crawled over to us," Brenda said, looking at Gerald.

Gerald's phone started ringing in his pocket. "Me too," he replied, pulling out his phone and looking at it. "It's Detective Stanley." He said as he put the phone on speaker and placed it on the table. "Good morning, Detective."

"Hello, Gerald."

"Hello, Detective, this is Glen. I'm with Gerald as well. Do you have any updates on my daughter's case?" I asked.

"Yes and no. That's the reason for my call. The blood on the clothing was Ciera's."

Sherry sobbed loudly, and Brenda immediately threw her hand over her mouth. Tears silently rolled down her cheeks. Gerald and I just stared at each other. Time stood still after hearing the words that sucked the air out of my chest. Sherry leaned over and cried in my chest. I hugged her tightly and caressed her back. Brenda did the same to Gerald. My sight was clouded with unshed tears, thinking back to the amount of blood that had soaked through those clothes. I shook my head in disbelief at the thought of my daughter out there suffering. What did she have to go through to lose that amount of blood? I didn't want to think about Ciera's dead body lying up somewhere, but after hearing this, I knew that it was a possibility. I've been hopeful but prepared for the worst since the day Ciera was missing.

"Gerald, I'm afraid I have to ask you, Brenda, and Brielle to come down to the station for questioning."

"What?" Brenda and Gerald exclaimed.

"You can't be serious." Brenda cried.

"What are you saying? We're suspects now?" Gerald yelled. "Detective, you can't possibly think we had something to do with our niece's disappearance."

"Gerald, you, your brother, and your company have helped me solve many cases. You should know it's not about what I think. It's about evidence… what can be proven. This is my job. I wouldn't be doing it right if I didn't follow through. In normal circumstances, I don't request interrogations over the phone. I hope you will cooperate with me and meet me at the precinct. If not, I'm right outside Glen's door."

Gerald remained quiet as he stared into my eyes, probably trying to find any doubt I had about him harming Ciera. I gave him a nod, letting him know that I got him. I knew he would never hurt

Ciera. There was never any doubt in my mind. I trusted my brother with my life.

"Alright, give us a moment to get our things," Gerald said. Luckily, they were already dressed. Brenda wore a grey oversized sweater with black skinny jeans and black boots. Her braids were up in a bun. Gerald wore blue jeans and a black long-sleeved shirt. Sherry and I were the only ones dressed in loungewear.

"Brielle's not with us. We'll have to call her to meet us down there." Brenda said.

"That's fine," Stanley replied.

"And we're not riding in your car," Gerald said sternly.

"I didn't think you would. Also, we have a warrant to search your home, Gerald."

"Oh, come on! You have got to be kidding me."

"No, This is no joking matter. This is protocol. You should have already expected this."

"Dammit," Gerald sighed. "Things seem to be getting worse and worse."

"It'll be alright, Gerald, go handle your business." I leaned into the phone. "Detective, make sure your people don't break the door down. Sherry and I will head down there to let them in."

"I'll pass on the message," Detective Stanly answered.

"Detective, give us five minutes. We'll be right out." Gerald said just before the detective disconnected the line.

Everyone scattered from the table, Sherry and I hurrying to get dressed. Five minutes later, Gerald tossed me his house key, and we were out the door. □

CHAPTER 15

Brayden

It's been forty-eight hours since Gerald and his family were summoned to the police station for questioning. I was confident that my planted evidence would ultimately result in Gerald's arrest. The mere thought of witnessing their downfall made me feel like a kid on Christmas. Couldn't nobody tear the smile off my face. All my hard work was about to pay off, and I wanted a front-row seat when the cops finally slapped them cuffs on his wrist.

Throughout the past week, I have devoted most of my time to being present at the office to stay well-informed about any developments and to procure Gerald's handprint. Sneaking around Glen's office proved to be a challenging task with Mike hanging around. Imagine my surprise when I found out this nigga had an office. Got me wondering just what it is his ass does around here.

I knocked on Glen's office door and patiently waited for his invitation to enter. In order to find out where his head was, I felt it was time to have a brief conversation with him.

"Come in," Glen said.

I opened the door and greeted him with a respectful "Hey, boss."

Glen was seated behind his desk, focused on an open file as he diligently typed away on the computer. He briefly glanced at me as I stepped forward, acknowledging my presence. "Long time no see, Brayden. How can I help you?" he didn't even crack a smile.

"I heard about what happened to Ciera. I wanted to offer my condolences. Is there anything I can do to help?" I asked as I took a seat in front of his desk.

Glen stopped typing and looked at me for a moment. "She's missing, not dead." He snapped.

"I was misinformed. I apologize," I said, looking down at the ground. It was the only thing I could do to hide the smile on my face. I took a deep breath and looked up. Glen was staring at me with a confused look on his face. "Is there anything I can do to help?" I coaxed.

"No, there's nothing you can do." He sighed. "Honestly, there's nothing that anyone can do." He said as he leaned back in his chair.

I was trying hard to make sure I didn't burst out laughing at his pathetic-looking ass. His expression was so comical that I could barely contain myself. "Are the cops any closer to finding her? Any leads?"

He shook his head no and wiped the stress from his eyes. "Enough about me. What brings you in today? Mike said he spoke with you. Are you ready for another assignment?"

"Ah… yeah, Mike already gave me a list of potentials. I'm trying to decide which one better fits my schedule."

Glen gave me a sly smirk. "Your schedule? I thought your availability was open. Did something change?"

"Hahaha," I laughed. "Actually, yeah. I finally grabbed myself up a shorty. Lucky for her, I'm thinking about wifing her up."

Glen nodded his head in approval. "I'm happy for you. Don't let this one slip away like the last one."

"Oh, I don't plan to. This one is on lockdown." I said seriously.

"Good for you, man."

A knock on the door caused us to both give our attention to Mike as he walked in, with Gerald following behind him. Gerald held two red folders in his hand. "Here's the files you were looking for." He said as he held them out for Glen.

"Thanks, man. These two are up for renewal, and Synergy added another location. Did Mark talk to you about placement?" Glen asked Gerald.

"Yeah. He's requesting six guards for a twelve-month contract and has already sent in his retainer along with the signed contract. I already sent him back his copy." Gerald replied.

Gerald gave a nod, then turned his gaze back to me. "Well, Brayden, you can add that one to your list of potentials."

"Sure, when does the assignment start and where?" I asked.

"Two weeks from today, in Georgia. Forty-five an hour." Gerald answered me.

"Speaking of... Eddie J. is requesting security detail in Los Angeles. He's performing at the Crypto arena from the sixteenth through the eighteenth of next month." Mike said.

I nodded my head, "Not bad. Let me think about it, then get back to you."

"Alright."

Mike cleared his throat, "Ay, I'm about to head out for the day. I set up the schedule. Kim will be printing them out as well as emailing everyone." He said. Gerald had a confused look.

"What schedules?" Gerald questioned.

"The sparring schedules. I made it mandatory." Mike answered.

Just what the hell is Mike doing around here? I thought to myself.

"Mr. Taylor," Kim said as she knocked on the door. "Detective Stanley is here for you." She said as she peeked through the cracked door.

"Thank you, let him in," Glen said.

Detective Stanley walked in with officers Romo and Levi. "Good afternoon, gentleman." I turned my gaze to Glen just in time to see him sneer the moment he laid eyes on Levi. "What the hell is he doing here? I was told he wouldn't be on this case." Glen grunted. Levi ignored him and kept his focus on the detective.

"I can assure you he's not. However, I'm here to make an arrest." Detective Stanely said before turning to Gerald. "Gerald, while searching your home, we found a bloody knife. Not only did it test positive for Ciera's blood, but your prints were also on the knife."

Gerald was taken aback. He slowly shook his head, denying the accusation. "The fuck outta here. That's impossible."

Glen stood up from his seat. His chair rolled back, hitting the wall. "Are you trying to tell me my daughter is dead? Did you find a body?"

Detective Stanley shook his head. "No Glen. No body has been found, but due to the evidence found against Gerald." He turned his gaze back to Gerald. "There has been a warrant issued for your arrest." Officer Romo walked towards Gerald with cuffs in her hands. Gerald lifted both hands, trying to keep them out of her reach.

"You don't want to do this, Gerald. You don't want to add resisting arrest to your charges, do you? Don't make this any harder on yourself." Levi said as he walked up to Gerald alongside Officer Romo. Gerald stood firm, his eyes unwavering.

"Yo, you can shut the fuck up and get the hell out of my office," Glen yelled at Levi. Levi's dumb ass looks at me, giving me a smirk. Then he turns back to Glen. "I'm just trying to help."

"We don't need your help. Officer Romo can handle this." Glen snapped. Levi stepped away, leaving Officer Romo to deal with the situation.

"What motive would I have to kidnap or hurt my niece? She's like a daughter to me." Gerald said to Detective Stanley.

"Plus, he was here when Ciera went missing," Glen added.

"Actually, he wasn't. According to security footage of this office. Gerald didn't arrive until after Ciera was abducted." The detective stated.

"That's because I was on my way here. I left home and came straight to work." Gerald argued.

"As far as I'm concerned, Gerald, you had means and opportunity. Officer Romo, cuff him. Gerald, you have the right to remain silent..."

"Man, this is bullshit!" Gerald shouted, holding his arms above his head as he dodged Officer Romo's grasp.

The detective continued. "Anything you say can be used against you..."

"Brah, don't resist. Just go with them. I swear man, I will get you out." Glen told Gerald.

Gerald yelled out in frustration as he turned around and dropped his arms behind his back. Gerald let Officer Romo cuff him and guide him out of the office, followed by Levi and the detective, who was still speaking. "...you have the right to an attorney..."

Gerald yelled from the hallway, "This is bull shit! Glen, call Brenda!"

"I'm already on it!" Mike shouted, holding his cell phone to his ear. I didn't even realize his ass was still in the room. That's one thing I hated about him. He was always in stealth mode, watching and observing.

I followed as Officer Romo pushed Gerald out of the building and towards the patrol car. A few people were in the lobby as Gerald was forced out of the building. Surprisingly, nobody took out their cell phones. The look of confusion and shock on their faces as they watched the scene unfold gave me a feeling of triumph. I stood just outside the door of the building as I watched my plan unfold before my eyes. I looked around the parking lot, noticing my next plan was set in motion. I had to bite my cheek to stop the smile from forming.

I glanced at Levi as he got into the patrol car. He kept a straight face, giving me a slight nod. I shook my head at how easy it was for him to play both sides. I looked back at the building, my gaze lingering on the glass door, and I watched the moment Mike and Glen turned down the hall back towards Glen's office.

I took a deep breath, trying to contain my excitement. I loved the smell of victory in the afternoon. I got just what I wanted: a front-row seat. As Levi's patrol car drove off, I walked to my car feeling victorious and anxious for what was to come.

CHAPTER 16

Ciera

"Argh," I moan from the pain of trying to lift myself up from the mattress. "Brayden!" I whispered. It wasn't meant to be a whisper.

I wanted to yell out his name, but I felt so weak. The most I can do is whisper. I'd lost count of how many days I'd been held captive. It was useless to remember if the few little specks of sunlight I saw on the floor were the present day or yesterday. My memory was sketchy, probably due to me passing out often. I've been beaten, raped, and starved daily... I think. I welcome the blackouts. It's the only peace I know.

Each day in captivity has blurred into the next, a monotonous cycle of fear and uncertainty. With each new day, the walls seem to close in more and more. When I think about it, I'm grateful he covered the windows. The thought of being taunted with glimpses of the outside world would drive me crazy. Being able to see the sunlight beaming down and not being able to feel it. I can't remember the last time I felt the sun's warmth on my skin or the wind blowing through my hair.

"Brayden!" I called out again, with a little more force. It probably sounded more like a moan this time.

I struggled to lift my arm, trying to reposition myself. There is a constant burning pain coming from both my wrists and ankles. I figured my skin must be raw underneath the shackles. My sweating made the pain worse.

The lack of ventilation was evident in the small room as the air remained stagnant and unpleasant. The absence of fresh air made the room feel hot, stale, and stuffy. Despite the oppressive atmosphere, a fan stood silent in the corner, offering a glimmer of hope for some relief. However, reaching it was impossible.

Brayden never bothered to turn on the fan. He'd say I didn't deserve such comfort. I wasn't allowed to go to the bathroom because that would mean I had to remain unchained. Instead, he would put absorbent pads under me. I haven't taken a shower since the day I was taken. Brayden would toss a bucket of cold, soapy water on me, then dry me up as he cussed me out about how bad I smelt before he forced his way into my body.

My mind drifted to Keon and how much I missed him. I missed his handsome face, the thick, gentle curve of his lips, and his chiseled biceps. I would give anything to feel his strong arms wrapped around me again. I wondered if he'd moved on or was out searching for me. Are my parents searching for me? Is Brielle still planning her wedding? What if everyone has moved on already? I cried myself to sleep at the pain of being forgotten.

I woke up to Brayden carrying me bridal style in a dimly lit room. The room I was forced to stay in remained dark. The light was coming in from just outside the door. I was too weak to hold my neck up. I had no choice but to lean my head on his shoulders. I'd hoped he would take me outside for some fresh air, but that was short-lived once I noticed he was headed to the bathroom.

He gently placed me in the tub and leaned my head against the back of the tub. This is it... He's going to drown me. I thought to myself as I followed his movements with my eyes. I welcomed it. I was ready for death. I figured I'd make this easy on him since I was too weak to fight back.

He turned on the shower head, and my muscles tensed slightly at the feel of cold water hitting my skin. I watched him as he walked out of the bathroom and out of sight. The water quickly heated up, causing my muscles to relax, and the steam made me feel weaker. How can something that feels so good also feel like it's sucking the life out of me? I closed my eyes and dozed off again.

The gentle scrubbing of a washcloth on my skin and the smell of caress soap woke me up. I stared at Brayden in the darkness, barely able to see his face.

"Did you ever love me?" I whispered.

I know he heard me because he paused for a second as if to think about his answer. Without answering, he continued to scrub me down without even giving me eye contact.

"Whatever I did to deserve this… I'm sorry." I whispered.

Again, he ignored me.

After washing me, he rinsed me, turned the shower off, and carried me back to the mattress. I noticed there were towels laid out over the mattress. He must have changed the pads because I didn't smell the stench of urine. I was thankful for that. I had to admit, it felt nice to finally be clean. I couldn't care less about oil or lotion at the moment.

"Your funeral is tomorrow." He said, breaking the silence as he laid me down.

"Huh?" I said, confused. I wasn't sure if I had heard him correctly.

"Your funeral is tomorrow morning. Your family thinks you are dead in case you wondered if a search party was out for you."

"But how? I'm right here." I said as tears rolled down my cheeks. They are moving on without me, I thought to myself. "Just... let me go, let me go to them!" I said in a broken voice.

"Do you hear yourself right now? If you showed up at your own funeral, you would give your parents a heart attack." He laughed.

"Why are you doing this?"

"Because you belong to me. Did you think I would sit by and watch you cuddle up to the next nigga? Plus... Your uncle killed my brother, and I think it's only fair that he sees how it feels to have somebody he loves taken away from him."

"What does that have to do with me? Brielle is his heart, not me!" I tried to shout, but it came out a little more than a whisper. I would never throw my cousin under the bus, but I wanted to know why I had to suffer for her father's sins.

"Don't underestimate yourself, Ciera. Gerald loves you more than you know. And Brielle, ... let's just say she's probably breathed her last breath already. Imagine going to a funeral the day after losing your only daughter." He laughed as he left the room, leaving me in just a sheet.

I knew better than to expect clothing. After waking up naked after our first fight, he made it clear that I wasn't allowed to wear clothes. He claimed that was no longer a necessity that I needed.

I still felt weak from the shower as I lay on the mattress, hurt and angry at what Brayden had admitted. I was too weak and tired to shed any more tears, although I was hurt to hear about Brielle dying. He could have at least told me how she died. We'll be together again soon enough. I whispered. How could my family give up on me? I hadn't even been gone that long. At least, I didn't think so. I had no idea what day or time it was. None of this would have happened if

Brayden wasn't so damn selfish and stubborn. Our breaking up was his own fault for ignoring me.

Brayden walked back in, carrying a plate. "Here's breakfast, lunch, and dinner." He said as he placed the plate on the floor near the head of the mattress. I looked down, barely able to see the contents. A slice of bread, a slice of cheese, and an apple. I didn't say anything. I doubt I would even eat it since I no longer felt hunger pains. Without another word, Brayden sat me up against the wall and reached for the shackles.

"Please, no…" I pleaded. "I'll be good. Please don't shackle me."

"You know… If you just submit to me, things would be much easier for you." He said as he chained up my left wrist. "You could finally be free of these chains for good. Of course, there would be some rules in place. But first, you have to earn my trust." He said as he finished chaining up my other wrist.

Instead of chaining up my ankles, he grabbed me and dragged me down to the center of the mattress. "You ready to show me how thankful you are for that shower?" he asked as he unzipped his pants. "You do a good job. I may unchain you."

I shook my head no, trying to keep my mouth closed as he tried to force himself into my mouth. He gripped my hair and pulled my head back so hard I cried out. The moment I felt his member in my mouth, I bit down.

"Argh!" He shrieked as he pulled out of my mouth. He punched me so hard that my head slammed into the wall. I heard something crack. I wasn't sure if the sound was my skull or the wall cracking. I felt something leaking down the side of my face. It had to be blood. I was in a daze. I knew what was happening, but I felt confused, and everything moved in slow motion.

"Dumb bitch!" He yelled as he pulled me down further on the mattress, causing me to fall to my back.

He sounded like he was miles away. I felt the moment he spread my legs open. I tried to scream, but no words would come out. I tried to close my legs and kick him away, but no matter how hard I tried, I couldn't control my limbs. I blacked out when I felt the pain of him forcing himself inside me. Hopefully, the darkness will be permanent this time since my family already thinks I'm dead. I'm tired of living. Maybe it is time to let go and make my death a reality.

☐

CHAPTER 17

Brayden

I stepped out of the shower, water droplets trickling down my body as I reached for a towel to dry off. I proceeded to dry my face and hair when I heard my phone ping from the sink. Curious, I swiftly wrapped the towel around my waist and made my way toward the sink. It turned out to be a notification informing me that my Uber Eats order was scheduled to arrive shortly.

Eager to be ready for the delivery, I swiftly put on a pair of comfortable boxers, my gray robe and slid into my Nike slides. I had placed an order for Nana's fried Chicken. I ordered the classic fried chicken, greens, macaroni and cheese, cornbread, and peach cobbler for dessert. My mouth watered just thinking about it, making my stomach growl in anticipation.

I waited by the window, watching for the Uber Eats driver to pull up. After two minutes of waiting, I walked out onto my front porch and checked my phone for an update. I swear if this Sam guy delivers my food to the wrong fuckin address, I'mma beat his ass! I thought to myself out loud. Another minute passed before a white Jeep Wrangler pulled up in front of my house. I walked to the edge of the driveway meeting the driver as he got out with my food in his hand.

"Sam, what the fuck man! I've been waiting for like five minutes." Sam's eyes got big at my response.

"I... I'm sorry, I got turned around."

"Haven't your dumb ass ever heard of GPS? Give me my damn food man!" I said as I snatched my two bags from out his hands. "Got me waiting out her for five fuckin minutes. Get the hell on!"

"What about your drink?" He asked, still holding it out to me.

"You drink that shit. I don't know what the fuck you did to it," I said, walking away. I turned around after hearing a plop-splash sound. This motherfucker threw the drink on the ground.

"Ay!" I yelled as he got in the jeep and drove off. All I could do was shake my head. I shrugged it off and went into the house with my food.

After settling down on the couch, I opened the bag and pulled out my containers of southern greatness. I opened the container, admiring the smell and sight of this perfectly cooked food. My mouth watered immediately before digging in. I hopped up and ran to the kitchen for my hot sauce and a cold bottle of beer.

I turned on the ten o'clock news as I devoured my dinner. Besides dealing with that jackass of a delivery driver, I was still in a good fuckin mood. Everything was going exactly as planned. There was a certain satisfaction I got from watching shit go down from the sideline, and it was icing on the fuckin cake. The untouchable Taylors finally got touched, and as a result, their family was falling apart.

I gotta admit, Gerald going away for the disappearance of Ciera wasn't part of my original plan. I wanted him dead. I still plan on offing him, but now it will be from inside his cell. I'll wait until after his sentencing to tell him about his little family secret, then I'll have someone shank his ass. I'm sure Levi will be of help with that.

As for Glen. I'll let him die without the satisfaction of knowing what happened to Ciera. Ciera will never again step foot outside these walls. Once I break her ass down. I'll build her into the submissive woman that I originally wanted her to be. All she needs to do is cook, clean, and spread them legs when I tell her. Maybe even raise a couple of my offspring. I'll spare the lives of Brielle, Brenda, and Sherry. Once I move Ciera out of the State. They'll never see her ass again.

I turned the volume up as my awaited segment started to play. A clip showcased Gerald being escorted to a police cruiser with his hands cuffed behind his back. I couldn't help but burst into laughter. "Aye Ciera! Your uncle is on the news!" I shouted, knowing she couldn't hear me. '...Talk about your family drama! Part owner of Diamond Watch Securities, Gerald Taylor, was arrested today for the kidnapping and possible murder of his niece, Ciera Taylor. Sources say that bloody clothing and a weapon were found in Gerald's home. No body has been found. As of now, Ciera Taylor is still missing, and Gerald Taylor denies any wrongdoing...'

"Yeah!" I laughed, raising my beer bottle as if to offer a toast to the TV screen, "My boy came through. I didn't even see his ass recording." I said out loud.

Now I'm about to hit that money! Damn, I wish Mason was here. I would love to see him tell Gerald who he really is. If only I could get a do-over, go back in time, and stop Mason from breaking into Gerald's home when he did. He would be on top right along with me. Mason may not be here physically, but his spirit was definitely with me.

☐

CHAPTER 18

Brielle

Oh my God! Could time move any slower? I thought as I looked back at the clock for the tenth time in thirty seconds. It's been a whole month since Ciera's been missing and two weeks since my dad has been arrested for the kidnapping and possible murder of my cousin.

I looked around the theater-style classroom, watching intently all the faces that were focused on the professor. I glanced down at their papers, noticing the full pages of notes that were written down. My gaze turned downwards to my own blank paper. I looked at the instructor, following her with my eyes. I know she's talking, but I can't hear a word she's saying. All I can hear is the ticking of the clock that I'm sitting near. What's the point of coming to class. With everything going on right now, there is no way I could concentrate.

The sudden movement of bodies in the classroom slamming their books closed and standing up caused me to look back at the clock for the umpteenth time. I felt a sense of relief, grateful that class was over. I folded up my blank paper and stuffed it in the side pocket of my backpack along with my pen. I fished around my bag for my keys as I walked towards the door.

The moment I crossed the door frame, I felt out of breath. A tingling feeling shot down my arms and legs. I had to lean against the wall to avoid falling as people continued to pour out of the classroom. This feeling immediately brought back memories the moment I looked up and spotted CeCe coming out of the same classroom. I didn't know that CeCe and I shared a classroom. She wore her white hoodie with light blue writing and light blue jeans. The same outfit that was found bloody at my house.

I immediately started following her. I called out to her, wishing she could hear me. I watched a man wearing a black hoodie and jeans follow closely behind her. I raced in front of her, then turned around to face her as I walked backward, keeping up with her pace. I caressed the side of her ice-cold face after noticing her horror look. My eyes blurred with tears when I stepped to the side and noticed the gun pointed at her back as she slowly walked in front of me.

I felt helpless. My cousin was terrified, and there was nothing I could do. I got a good look at her kidnapper's face, hoping that I recognized him, but I didn't. I started to panic once I noticed CeCe's car coming into view as we walked towards it. I remembered the vehicle description of the SUV she was taken in. Thanks to our nightly drives, trying to spot this car.

I ran ahead, seeing the SUV parked next to CeCe's car, just like I was told there were no license plates on the vehicle. I walked quickly around the SUV to see if I noticed anything that could be useful. I watched through the driver's window of the SUV as CeCe tossed her cell on the ground.

I stood frozen, sobbing and watching as CeCe was forced into the back seat of the SUV. I screamed out, "Noo!" when he stabbed her in the neck, and she fell onto the backseat, knocked out. Time was running out. I quickly scanned the car again, looking for anything to help us locate her. My eyes settled on the vin number as he walked behind the vehicle. I grabbed my pen and paper from the side pocket of my backpack and wrote the number as quickly as possible. By the time he started to reverse the car, I'd just finished copying the last five digits. I glanced at CeCe one last time, screaming her name as he drove off.

Seeing my cousin lying down, looking as though she had died, broke me down. I didn't know if that would be the last time I saw my cousin alive, and the look of terror on her face tore me up. I screamed for her until I had no breath left. I dropped to my knees and closed my eyes as I tried to fight through the pain in my chest, but now Ciera's frightened face was the only thing I saw when I closed my eyes. It caused me to sob harder.

"Brielle!" I heard someone yell as I was lifted off the ground. I opened my eyes to find I was just outside the classroom door.

"Brielle! Are you okay?" I turned my head to find Keon looking me over. "What happened? Did somebody hurt you?" he asked, quickly looking around us. I instantly threw my arms around him and cried on his shoulder.

"Shh, calm down, Brie. I gotchu… Tell me what happened."

"I-I… saw CeCe?"

"What! Where?" he pushed me away, looking around frantically. "Where did you see her?"

"Sh-she came… out of the classroom and…. Went towards the parking lot." I stuttered while pointing towards the parking lot. He let me go, getting ready to go in the direction I pointed. I quickly grabbed his hand. "Keon, wait!" He looked at me with irritation.

"What Brie, she's getting away!"

"No… Keon… it's not what you think." I said, still sobbing.

"Brielle, what the hell are you talking about? I need to go after her!" he urged.

"Just listen!" I yelled. Not caring about the people staring at us as they passed by. I told Keon about my ability to go into the past and what I saw. Once I finished, I didn't know if he was angry or disappointed or if he even believed me.

"What the hell, Brielle! Are you shit'in me right now?"

"No!"

"You were dreaming, Brielle. Listen… I love you like a sister, but this shit ain't funny," he said, walking away. I stemmed forward, grabbed his arm, and spun him around.

"Really Keon! You picked me up off the ground while I was bawling my eyes out. What in the hell would make you think I was sleeping ON THE GROUND!" I yelled.

Keon sighed, "Brielle… you described exactly what was on the video footage." He said, rubbing the stress from his face with both hands.

"What video footage?" I asked.

"The security footage of Ciera being kidnapped."

"I wasn't told anything about a video. Look!" I said, handing him the paper.

"What is this?" he asked, taking the paper from me.

"It's the VIN number I got from his truck." Keon had a shocked expression on his face as he looked at the number.

"How did you…" His words trailed off.

"I told you I saw her."

"Did you see his face?"

"Yes, but he wasn't someone I recognized."

"And you're sure you got the VIN to the right car?"

I smacked my lip. "I'm sure it's the right vehicle. My cousin was laid out in the back seat as I wrote it down." Silent tears fell from my eyes at the mention of her. He tapped the paper as he was thinking.

"This could work… I know someone who might be able to help us get a lead on Ciera."

"Really! I said, hopeful. "You sure… I mean, I could just give it to my dad."

"Your dad is locked up, Brie."

"Oh yeah, I forgot."

"Don't worry about it. I'll take care of it." He said, taking a few steps back. "Just don't tell anyone about this… not yet. I'll keep you posted." He yelled as he was running off.

I gave him a nod, knowing I didn't have enough voice to yell back. Being alone suddenly and watching the eyes that stayed fixed on me had me feeling embarrassed. They had no idea why I was going hysterical. I looked around as I tugged on my backpack. I spotted a girl looking at me with her face scrunched up in a scowl. She was leaning against the side of the building before taking off in the direction of Keon. I hoped Keon knew what he was doing. I gave him my only copy, and I wasn't sure if I could go back in time again.

☐

CHAPTER 19

Keon

I drove home like a bat out of hell, my heart pounding in my chest. Once again, the urgency of the situation pushed my classes to the back burner. Ciera was my main priority. She will always be number one, no matter what's going on in my life. The adrenaline rushed through my veins as I maneuvered my car with precision, swerving in and out of lanes. The sound of horns blaring and tires screeching filled the air. I kept my eyes peeled for any signs of flashing lights. I couldn't afford any distractions from law enforcement. The way I felt right now could very well end up in a high-speed chase.

This has been one hell of a month. It started with me carrying around an engagement ring, feeling the weight of its significance burning a hole in my pocket. Now, all I want to do is blow a hole in somebody's chest for touching my woman. I've been checking in with Glen and Sherry often for updates, but every update I get seems to be worse than the last. Now Gerald is in jail for a crime I know he didn't commit. The evidence they found is scary as hell, but I won't believe Ciera's dead... not until they have a body and I identify it myself.

The blaring sound of a horn honking snapped me out of my thoughts just in time to notice the car in front of me abruptly hit its brakes and quickly switched lanes to avoid colliding with the vehicle in front. Reacting swiftly, I instinctively slammed my foot on the brake pedal, bringing my own car to a halt inches away from the vehicle that would have been responsible for the collision.

While waiting for the light to change, I took the crumbled paper out of my pocket and stared at the VIN number. The things Brielle told me about going into the past left me speechless. I mean... it's impossible. Seeing her on the ground crying scared the hell out of me. I thought someone hurt her. Then she gave me a VIN number...a fuckin VIN number. My mind is blown.

Fifteen minutes later, I find myself hurrying up the stairs towards my apartment, the adrenaline still pumping through my veins. As I reach my door, I quickly unlock it and slam it shut behind me. Without wasting any time, I make a beeline for my room, my heart still racing from the urgency of the situation. With a swift motion, I toss my bookbag onto the bed, not caring where it lands. My focus is solely on finding my black duffle bag, which I know is hidden under the bed. I drop to the floor and stretch my arm out, feeling around for the familiar touch of the bag.

Finally, my fingers brush against the smooth fabric of the duffle bag. I grab hold of it and pull it towards me. Sitting back on the edge of the bed, I begin to rummage through the bag, emptying its contents onto the bed. Socks, clothing, and paperwork are scattered across the bed. My eyes are fixed on one thing: the little black box that my dad had sent me.

My dad worked for the CIA. Because of the secretive nature of his work, he would send Jessica and me a burner phone and a phone number with where to reach him every couple of months. Our phone calls had to be quick and to the point. Jessica doesn't know what our dad did for a living. All she knew was that he traveled frequently for work. Our dad deliberately kept the details of his profession hidden from her and our mothers to protect them from the potential risks and dangers associated with his line of work. However, for some reason, he trusted me with that information.

I pulled out the black box and eagerly opened it. A flip phone lay nestled inside with a yellow post-it note on top, his phone number written down. I powered on the phone and entered the number my dad provided. I'm sure he would know who was calling. He always saved our assigned numbers before shipping us our phone. After a few seconds, the phone began to ring. On the third ring, my dad answered the call.

"Yeah," He greeted.

"Pops"

"Son… it's not a good time."

"Not for me either," I answered.

"What's going on?"

"Ciera's been kidnapped." There was a quick pause while he took in my words.

"…As of when?"

"Last month."

"Shit! That's not something I was expecting to hear. How are you holding up?"

"Not good Dad," I answered honestly.

"Any leads?"

"Originally, no, but I just came across the VIN number today."

"Vehicle?"

"Black Dodge Durango, newer model. Not sure on the year."

"Give me the VIN." After taking down the number, I heard him inhale deeply. "Keep this phone on you."

"Thanks, pops."

"Love ya…" CLICK… The line disconnected before I could say it back.

I woke up to a rapid knocking on the door. Startled, I quickly realized that I must have dozed off, as I noticed the time on my watch was three o'clock. It dawned on me that I've been asleep for three hours; honestly, it was the best sleep I've had in a month. The newfound hope I felt probably had something to do with it. I groan as I get up to answer the door. I was irritated that someone had the audacity to come over without calling first. Not many people knew where I lived other than Jessica, Ciera, and her family, and neither would come over without calling first.

I snatched the door open, not bothering to glance through the peephole. To my astonishment, Leilani was standing right in front of me. She wore blue jeans, a black crop top, and black sandals. She clutched a cardboard cupholder with two drinks in one hand while the other held a greasy brown bag of food. I'm not going to lie. The smell emanating from that bag made my stomach growl.

"Surprise!" She laughed as she tried to make her way into my apartment. I blocked her with my body.

"What the hell are you doing?"

Her smile widened as she held up the food and drinks. "Duh, isn't it obvious babe? I bought lunch."

"Don't call me babe," I growled. "It's Keon… You're lucky I don't make your ass call me Mr. Wright. How do you know where I live?"

"I will call you whatever you want me to." She flirted.

I sighed, putting one hand on the door frame and holding the door with the other. "You still didn't answer my question."

"Oh my god, Keon! If you must know, Jessica told me." She said, smacking her lips.

"Jessica told you," I repeated, not believing one word coming out of her mouth.

"That's what I said."

I closed the door in her face, locking it before calmly walking back to my room to get my phone. Leilani began kicking the door. "Really Keon! Open the damn door. The fries are getting cold... Keon!" She shouted.

I went to my room and grabbed my cell phone off the bed. I dialed Jessica's number and anxiously waited for her to pick up. As I stood there, the sound of continuous pounding on the door echoed through the room. Shaking my head, I tried to focus on the phone call, hoping Jessica would answer soon. Hey, you've reached Jessica.... I hung up and redialed her number. This time, she picked up on the first ring.

"Keon! Please tell me you got an update." She blurted out.

"What, you screening calls now? Why didn't you answer the first time I called?"

"No stupid. I just got out of the shower. Now answer me already. Did they find my friend?"

I sighed, "No, sorry lil sis. No update as of yet."

She let out a breath and remained quiet. I let her have a moment since I know how it feels to answer the phone with hope and prayed that someone was calling with good news. I didn't want to tell her about the possible lead in case it led to another dead end.

"Ay, Jessie, did you tell Leilani where I lived?"

"Hell no! I don't talk to that thirsty bitch."

I laughed as I took quick strides to the door. Leilani was still yelling from the other side. I unlocked it and snatched the door open. Leilani jumped.

"Hey, Jessie… Can you repeat that?" I asked with a straight face, putting the phone on speaker.

"I said hell no, I haven't spoken to that thirsty bitch."

"I know she's not talking about me!" Leilani said.

"Who's that?" Jessica asked.

"That would be Leilani. She showed up at my place and said you gave her the address." I knew Jessica wouldn't care if I put her on speaker in front of Leilani. Even though Jessica is my younger sister, she doesn't play when it comes to her big brother. She never liked Leilani from the start.

"What? It wasn't enough that you slept with my dad. Now you're stalking my brother?" Jessica yelled through the phone.

"That's between me, your brother, and your daddy. You just better watch how you speak to me."

"Do you hear how dumb you sound right now-"

"No Keon! You don't say shit to her. Aye, Chica, You better watch for me on these streets. Better yet, come see me since you want to show up at people's homes unannounced. 267 S. Walburg Ln. Come see me, 'cause I got something for your stank ass."

"You can take your food and bounce," I added before closing the door in her face.

"Ugh, I hate her!" Jessica screamed. "How did she even find you?"

I walked back to my room and took a seat on my bed. "I think she followed me from school. Unfortunately, I have a class with her."

"Sucks for you," Jessica said.

"I'll be okay."

"Alright Mano, keep me posted. I have to get ready for work."

"I will. Later, sis," I said before the line went dead.

I scanned the room, my eyes landing on the burner phone on my bed. Curiosity piqued, I reached out and flipped it open, checking for any missed calls. To my disappointment, there were none. As I closed the phone, I slipped it into my back pocket and decided to occupy myself with cleaning. Truth be told, I was desperately searching for something to distract myself from thoughts of Ciera. It had only been three hours since I last spoke to my dad, but already I could feel the weight of waiting. Patience was never my strong suit.

☐

CHAPTER 20

Brielle

Ciera's booming sound of 'Level up' resonated through the gym speakers. I was the only one in the gym today, and I was grateful for that. I wasn't in the mood to socialize, so having the space was a relief. Sweat trickled down my face as I pounded away at the heavy bag. I felt the tension leaving my body with each punch and kick combination.

Normally, I make it a point to work out at least twice weekly to stay in shape for my upcoming nuptials. However, this past week has been different. It seems like I've been here every day, using the gym as an outlet for the storm my family is currently going through. Finding solace in physical activity has always been CeCe's go-to method of coping with difficult times. A small smile escapes my lips as I finally realize why she always seemed stress-free.

"Argh!" I screamed in anguish as I delivered more punches and kicks to the heavy bag. Every muscle screamed in protest as I pushed myself harder. My whole body was on fire, aching from exertion. I knew my body would cramp up if I didn't stop soon. Gasping for breath, I averted my eyes to the clock on the wall. I've been working out for an hour and a half. The rhythmic beats of Kendrick Lamar's 'Humble' started playing as I looked around the gym, sweat dripping from my brow. I realized that I had gone through almost every workout equipment available. The weight machines, treadmills, the rowing machines, stairs- I had conquered them all. My goal was to make my muscles burn enough to take my mind off witnessing Ciera's kidnapping. The haunting image kept replaying in my head, and I had to do something to escape it.

I turned off the Bluetooth on my phone, silencing the music coming from the speakers in the gym. I bent down, picked up my pink Under Armour gym bag from the floor, and swiftly threw the strap over my shoulder, ready to shower. As I walked down the hallway towards the locker room, I was taken aback when I unexpectedly ran into Mike. Uncle Glen told me he was back in town, but our paths hadn't crossed until now. Whenever I came to the office to work out, I missed him, or he was in a meeting. From the looks of it, he was still in a meeting. Mike had his back turned towards me while he spoke to someone else. I'm guessing another employee.

I decided against interrupting their conversation and went straight to the locker room. As I entered, I tossed my bag on the bench and took a moment to relax. Standing up, I began to do a little stretching. While I focused on my thoughts, I could faintly hear Mike's conversation with the other person.

…"I understand what's going on around here, and honestly, it doesn't concern you." Mike said. I know his deep voice anywhere. Just like his physique, His deep baritone voice demanded respect.

"I know that, Mike. I just wanted to be available to help." Said the unknown voice.

"And how exactly are you helping by walking around the office? This is a place of business. There is work to be done. Speaking of, have you chosen a client yet?" asked Mike.

"No, I'm still weighing my options."

"It doesn't take that long to weigh no options. Listen. I'm giving you two days to pick a client, or we will have to talk about your employment status with us. You're sitting here with no work for the past month, yet you roam around this office like you are bored. This is not acceptable."

"I understand, Mike. It won't happen again. I'll get back to you in two days."

"Alright, Brayden. I'll catch you later."

I gasped at the name. "Brayden," I muttered under my breath. I got up and slowly cracked the door open hoping to get a glimpse of Ciera's ex. It seemed like everyone had seen him but me. I hoped to finally see him at the New Year's Eve party, but he never showed up. Curiosity got the better of me as I peered out onto the empty hallway. Dang, I missed him, I thought as I closed the door. "Oh well," I shrugged.

I turned the shower on, then quickly peeled off my sweaty clothes and stepped into the stream of water. The hot water cascaded over my body, instantly soothing my tired muscles. I switched the shower head to the massage setting, allowing the water to penetrate deep into my already tight muscles, gradually loosening them. After thoroughly lathering and rinsing my body, I stepped out of the shower, drying myself off. I grabbed a bottle of baby oil gel from my duffle bag. I applied it generously, taking my time massaging it onto my skin, ensuring I got in a good stretch while moisturizing myself. Once done, I put on my green sweatpants and a black t-shirt that read 'Try Me.'

After packing up my items, I walked out of the locker room. I decided to find Uncle Glen and let him know I was leaving. Out of habit, I went to my dad's office, but I was surprised to find my mom sitting at the desk, engrossed in work.

"Mama… what are you doing here?" I asked, leaning onto the door frame.

"Oh, hey honey. I'm just trying to help out as much as I can. I don't want your dad backed up with work. Plus, Glen is going crazy trying to put out this fire." She answered as she filed some paperwork.

"What fire?"

"You haven't seen the news?"

"No. What happened."

She huffed as she shook her head. "Somehow, someone recorded your dad getting arrested and sent it to the news."

"What!" I huffed.

"Yeah girl. Now we have clients sending back guards and trying to break their contracts."

"Oh my God," I said, rubbing my forehead. I couldn't stand by and watch my dad and Uncle's business go down the drain.

"Don't worry, it's called a contract for a reason. Plus, your dad is innocent. The truth will come out eventually. It has to." She said as she pushed the drawer closed to the file cabinet.

"Is there anything I can do to help?"

"No. You have enough on your plate. Speaking of... Any updates on Ciera?"

I knew she was asking if I went into the past. I wanted to tell her, but I told Keon I wouldn't. I'll wait to see if he comes through. "No, nothing yet. Are you going home tonight?"

"No. The house is still being repaired, and I don't want to be in that house without your dad... again."

"Well, I'm about to head out."

"Are you still staying with Loyal?" She asked, raising her eyebrow.

"Yeah."

"Alright. Don't pop up pregnant before the wedding."

"Mom!"

"Don't mom, me."

"Okay, byeee." I whined, now in a rush to finish this conversation.

"Bye" she said as I closed the office door.

I continued down the hall towards Uncle Glen's office. I passed Mike's office and gave him a quick wave, and he returned with a nod. I finally caught him alone, and I don't even feel like talking to him. I thought as I continued past his door. I reached Uncle Glen's office and knocked before slowly cracking the door open.

"...I appreciate your concern and your patience... yes... eighteen years to be exact." Uncle Glen spoke into the receiver. "Uh Derreck... I don't know what to tell you other than Gerald is innocent. However, you still have a two-year contract..." I waved goodbye to him when he finally looked up from the computer, giving me eye contact. He waived back. I closed the door and headed to Loyal's place.

After the twenty-minute drive to Loyal's and Trust's place, I started to regret my intense workout. The muscles in my body were aching, and I could feel the fatigue setting in. I hadn't realized how sore I was until I stepped out of the car and began to make my way up the three flights of stairs to get to Loyal's unit. I fumbled for the key as I approached their door. The door swung open just as I was about to insert the key into the keyhole. Trust was standing before me, wearing a black suit and turtleneck shirt.

"Oh! Hey Brie," he smiled.

"What's up Trust? You're heading out again?"

"Yeah." He laughed. "I got business to attend to." He said as he stepped to the side, allowing me to walk through.

"Mmmm… It smells good in here." I said as the mouth-watering aroma hit me.

"That's your man in there, throw'in down in the kitchen. How are you holding up?" he asked, referring to my family drama. I just shrugged my shoulders. Trust wrapped his arms around me, hugging me tightly. "Keep your head up lil sis. Ciera will turn up, and your dad can hold his own. He'll be okay."

I responded the only way I could. "Thanks," I said, giving him a weak smile. He squeezed me tighter right before letting me go and gave me a quick peck on the forehead.

"Alright. I'll catch y'all later," Trust said as he walked out the door, closing it behind him.

From my vantage point in the living room, I saw Loyal clearly as he worked his magic at the stove. This was a basic bachelor's pad. The living room had a black leather loveseat and sofa, a brown coffee table in the middle of the room, and a flat screen TV mounted to the wall. One picture was hanging on the wall, a silhouette of a man with a gold crown on his head.

Two black bar stools separated the family room and the eat-in kitchen. The cabinets were beige, complemented by white countertops and matching appliances. Their place was clean and well-maintained. However, it was evident that a feminine touch was missing. Unfortunately, it would remain that way because I was not living here once we were married.

I walked into the kitchen with the weight of my duffle bag hanging from my shoulder. I approached Loyal from behind and wrapped my arms around him as I leaned to the side to catch a glimpse of what he was cooking. I looked up at him, seeing his gaze on me, his lips crashed against mine.

"Hey beautiful." He greeted. "How was your day?"

"Long," I responded. "It smells good in here. What's cookin'?"

"Chicken teriyaki. We still have about another thirty minutes until it's done. Why don't you go soak your body."

I didn't want to, being that I already took a shower, but the stiffness and aching of my muscles made me think that might be just what I needed to get some relief. "I think I might just do that." I stood on my tippy toes and gave him a peck on his cheek before walking away. I went into Loyal's room and tossed my duffle bag on the bed. I unzipped it, took out my sweaty gym clothes, and went to the hallway bathroom to throw it in his hamper.

The moment I entered the bathroom, a feeling of awe washed over me. The soft glow of candles illuminated the room. It wasn't an excessive amount of candles, but just enough to create a serene and relaxing environment. I noticed the bathtub filled with bubbles. The steam and the scent of lavender and eucalyptus rose from the water. On the far end of the tub was an open bag of Epsom salt. Man, I love this guy! I think to myself with a smile.

Knowing that I was staying with two men and was a clean freak, I switched on the light to ensure there were no dirt rings in the tub. I even ran my fingers down the side of the tub. A sense of relief washed over me at the feel of a smooth surface beneath my fingertips.

I turned off the light when I noticed Loyal's tablet propped up against the mirror. The screen displayed a playlist titled 'Wedding Playlist.' I smiled and pressed play. I didn't even know Loyal had put a playlist together. I had slowed down on wedding plans when CeCe went missing. It oddly brought me comfort to know that Loyal was still taking care of some things.

The sensual sound of John Legend's 'All of Me' softly flowed through the tablet speakers as I removed my clothes, folded them, and placed them on the sink since they were still clean. I tossed my panties in the hamper and slowly placed my foot in the water. A tingling sensation ran up my spine at the heat from the water. It wasn't too hot but hot enough that I had to immerse myself slowly. Thankfully, I left a crack in the door. Finally relaxing, I leaned back against the tub, sinking down into the water, only leaving my neck and head out of the water. I closed my eyes, thinking of my wedding day as Jaheim's 'Never' began to play. Before I knew it, I had dozed off.

A rigid tapping on the door started me awake. I opened my eyes to see Loyal peeking in the bathroom.

"Babe, you alright in there?"

I yawned, sitting up in the tub. My water had cooled down slightly. "Yeah, I dozed off," I admitted, pulling the plug to the drain. Loyal grabbed my towel from the rack and held it open as I exited the tub.

"I figured. I told you thirty minutes until dinner. It's been forty-five."

"I'm sorry, I didn't realize how tired I was."

"Come on." He said, scooping me up bridal style. "I know what you need."

He carried me to the bedroom and gently laid me down before leaving the room. I took the time to dry myself off. Just as I finished, he returned with a bottle of massage oil. A smile escaped me as I turned around and face-planted onto the bed.

"I thought you would like this." He smiled.

I lay there anticipating his touch. I braced myself after hearing the lid snap on the bottle. The next thing I knew, my muscle tenseness and stress were melting away as he massaged every inch of my body. A soft moan escaped my lips at him, kneading my sore muscles. Once he finished, I turned over, and he started the process again. Somewhere between my fingers and my toes, sleep took over once again.

My eyes fluttered open at the feel of gentle kisses being planted all over my body. "All done," Loyal said in between kisses.

"Thanks. That felt good." I moaned.

"I know what else would make you feel good." He teased.

"No Loyal… We agreed that we would wait until after the wedding."

"Yeah, yeah, yeah… but there are other things we could do."

"Loyal!" I said, finally looking at him.

Imagine my surprise to see him as naked as the day he was born, his member standing at attention. I laughed as I grabbed my towel and rolled off the bed away from him. "When did this happen?" I laughed, covering myself up.

"What? I didn't think it was fair for you to be the only one naked. I did this for you." He grinned, walking towards me.

"No!" I laughed, leaping on the bed to get to the other side of the room. I grabbed his shirt off the nightstand and tried putting it on as fast as possible. Loyal laughed.

"What's that supposed to do? You can cover up your top half. It's the bottom half of your body I want."

"Loyal! We agreed to wait." I laughed, backing up into the corner.

"We didn't agree to anything. That was your saying, not mine. It's not like this is our first time." He said, still walking towards me.

"Loyal, please… this means a lot to me." I pleaded.

He groaned. "Fine. What kind of man would I be if I didn't at least try."

"Thanks babe!" I smiled.

"I shouldn't have said anything. I should have just done it." He mumbled, walking out of the room.

I laughed at the sight of him pouting. I was tempted, but I would never have told him that.

After cleaning myself up, I slid on some panties and shorts to go along with his T-shirt. With my loungewear on, I went to the kitchen to fix our plates while Loyal was in the bathroom.

To my surprise, he had already fixed our plates and placed them under a heat lamp. The delicious aroma of teriyaki chicken, white rice, and broccoli had my stomach growling. I poured both of us a glass of lemonade. Somehow, I managed to carry our plates and drinks back into the room without spilling anything. I carefully set the drinks on the nightstand and put our plates on the bed.

Loyal came out of the bathroom, wearing some light blue pants that hung just below the v-line. "You read my mind." He said, noticing the food on the bed. "What are we watching?"

"John Wick," I answered, setting the remote down.

We chatted on and off during the duration of the movie. I contemplated whether or not I should tell him about the new lead that could hopefully help us to find CeCe. My hesitation stemmed from the fact that I didn't want to reveal the way I acquired this lead. It pained me to keep secrets from Loyal. He was an open book, and so was I. I hope and pray we find CeCe and that Keon keeps how we got the lead between us.

☐

CHAPTER 21

Keon

I lay in bed staring at the popcorn ceiling of my bedroom, lost in thought as I watched the sunlight dance around on. I had another sleepless night thinking about what Ciera could be going through. Could she be held captive so close to me that I pass her by daily?

My stomach ached at the thought of my dad trying to get info from the VIN number. What if he returned with nothing or a lead that led to another dead end. "Ugh!" I grunted as I sat up at the edge of the bed. "Why is waiting so fuckin hard!" I screamed out.

I decided to skip class today. There was no way I could concentrate in school with all the what ifs running through my mind.

I grabbed the burner phone, taking it to the bathroom while freshening up. After my shower, I lotion myself and put on my gray acid-wash jeans and a black T-shirt. Headed to the kitchen I grabbed the remote off the coffee table turning on the news, hoping for some good news. Deciding I really didn't need to see the weather report I kept on track to make me some breakfast. .

While eating my meal of sausage and eggs, I started surfing channels when the burner phone rang. Quickly I put the TV on mute and stared at the phone for a moment. For some reason, I felt this call was as permanent as death. That one word from my dad could zap away all my hopes. I picked up the phone and slowly pressed the call button while I gulped down the food in my mouth. I spit the food in my mouth in a napkin, my appetite was suddenly gone.

"What's up Pops?"

"Hey son, how's it going?"

I sighed. "The suspense is killing me. I haven't slept in a month; I can't think or eat…"

"You sound like a man in love, son."

"I am. Did you find anything from the VIN number?" I asked with my eyes closed. I held my breath as I mentally prepared for his answer.

"Actually, I did. Got something to write with?"

"Hold on a minute." I jumped up before my mind could even register what he said. I ran to my room, gathered my pen and notebook off my dresser, and sat at the edge of my bed.

"Ready"

"The VIN number pulled up a Brayden Reed.

"Brayden!" I yelled.

"You know him?"

"I don't know him, but I know of him. If we're talking about the same guy, he works for Diamond Watch Securities. He's also Ciera's ex-boyfriend."

"I looked more into this Brayden fellow. It turns out he has three properties. One rental and two he owns. I had a couple of people from the area check out the properties. If he has Ciera, she would most likely be held at 3756 Blue Lantern Way."

I quickly wrote down the address. "What makes you think Ciera is being held there?"

"Well, the other property he owns looks to be rented out to a Beverly Goodard. She lives there with her husband and two small children. The rental property is empty. The lease is ending soon, so he may have moved out recently. The property he resides in was recently purchased in December."

"Alright"

"Now listen up, son. I'm not saying Ciera is there. All I'm saying is the owner of that vehicle lives there."

"I understand Pops. Damn, this man isn't going to let me check his property. I gotta find a way to get in there."

"Take this number down. 871-332-1178, ask for Nathan."

"Alright," I said, taking down the number. I repeated it back to him.

"This guy is known as a… problem solver. He'll help you as a favor to me. Just tell him Leon referred you. Tell him you're my son."

"Got it."

"Alright, I got to go. Keep me updated, and most importantly, be safe."

"Yes sir," I said before the line went dead. I immediately called Nathan. It rang a few times before he answered.

"Speak." His voice was dark and deep.

"I'm looking for Nathan."

"Who's looking for Nathan?"

"Keon. I was referred to you by Leon. I'm his son."

There was a brief moment of silence before he spoke again. "Meet me at the Crimson Marina. 7am tomorrow morning." Then the line went dead.

The following day, I arrived at the marina at 7 a.m. sharp. It was quiet and calm, with the morning overcast still visible. Occasionally, a little sunlight would break through, giving me a little taste of warmth.

I walked up and down the dock, unsure of who I was looking for. Other than myself, a father and son were out loading a small boat with fishing gear. I continued walking up and down the dock before returning to stand at the entrance to the marina.

"Keon!"

I turned around at the sound of my name. "Loyal?" I say in surprise. As I get ready to pull him into a bro hug. "What's up man? What are you doing out here this early?" I gave him a double back slap before releasing him.

He raised his fishing rods, "I always do my fishing in the morning. Hey, can you grab this for me?" Loyal said as he handed me his fishing rod and bucket. "Let me run to the car to get my cooler and some bags, be right back." He said as he ran off.

He moved so fast I didn't even get a chance to tell him I was waiting for someone. I glanced down at my watch. I've been waiting for almost five minutes. I scanned the parking lot one last time before following Loyal to his boat.

We stepped onto the drop platform, climbed a few stairs, and walked through an outdoor lounging area. I followed Loyal into the galley, and we put the items down on the counter.

"This is nice. is it yours?" I asked as I looked around.

"No, it's my mom's."

"Figures. The name of the yacht is Queen Bee." I chuckled. "So, what's up? You about to go fishing for dinner?"

Loyal chuckled. "Oh, you got jokes! What… do you think my life revolves around cooking?"

I shrugged. "I just know that's what you do. Ain't no shame in that."

"Naw man…" Loyal said, taking a seat at the bar. "Cooking is my outlet. It calms me."

I gave him a nod in understanding. "So, how's the wedding planning going?" I questioned, following Loyal into the common area and taking a seat on the sofa.

"Slow. Brielle's more focused on Ciera right now, which is understandable. Ciera's everyone's focus at the moment."

Hearing Ciera's name reminded me of the reason I was here. I looked at my watch. It was now twelve minutes past seven. I was late, and something told me that Nathan is not the type of guy you want to keep waiting. I stood up to leave.

"Brah... It was nice chatting it up with you, but I really need to get going…." My words faded as I noticed two men walking onto the boat, dressed casually in jeans and a t-shirt. Loyal turned around to see what had my attention.

"Oh, Keon, this is my brother Trust. Trust, you remember Keon. He was at the engagement party."

"Yeah!" He said as he dropped the bag and briefcase carefully on the floor. "Sup Keon, how you livin'?" he asked, giving me dap.

"I'm alright, you?"

"Good, good." He responded as he walked to the bar and pulled out a glass.

"And this is my father, Nathan," Loyal said, nodding towards his father.

My eyebrows furrowed together in a frown. "Nathan?"

"Keon, nice to meet you again," Nathan greeted. "Now, before we get into it, Trust, get us on the water," he commanded. "… and Keon have a seat." He said before walking in the common area.

I sat down in shock. I had no idea my father and Loyal's dad knew each other.

Loyal laughed. "You should see the look on your face." He said.

"Did you know our fathers knew each other?"

He shook his head no. "He called me early this morning and told me about this meeting. He figured you wouldn't remember him from the party."

"Did he know who I was at the party?"

"Hell no, but when you called and said your name was Keon... I mean, how many Keon's do you know?"

"Point taken. So, yawl go fishing a lot?"

"No, that's just a decoy. When we're talking business, we do it on the water. No risk of anyone hearing something they shouldn't."

After the boat stopped in the middle of the lake. Nathan and Trust joined Loyal and me in the salon. They took a seat on some chairs across from me. "So, what's going on?" Nathan asked me. "What's this about?"

"Ciera."

"Alright, you got my attention. What about her?" Nathan asked.

"Yesterday morning, I got a lead on the person who kidnapped her. I gave the info to my dad, who found the address where Ciera is most likely being held." I said, trying to be as vague as possible.

"Holy shit! Have you told anyone?" Trust asked.

"No. I didn't want to get anyone's hopes up if it was a dead end."

"I can understand that." Loyal said.

"What lead did you get," Nathan said.

"A VIN number," I replied.

"How did you get that?" Loyal asked.

"Brielle... She got the VIN number to the car." I answered.

"How the hell did Brielle end up with the VIN number?" Loyal asked.

"Honestly, brah, it's not my place to tell. You should talk to her." I answered. "but that's not the crazy part. Guess who the vehicle is registered to...Brayden Reed." I answered before giving him a chance to guess.

"What the fuck! Are you kidding me?" Loyal's response was the same as mine.

"Whose Brayden?" Trust asked.

"He works for Glen and Gerald. He's also Ciera's ex." Loyal answered.

Trust shook his head, "Damn. Right under our fuckin noses."

Nathan spoke up, "So let me guess. Leon expects me to go in and retrieve her as a favor to him?" Nathan asked.

"Yes, but we're not sure if Ciera is there. If he is working with someone else, it's a possibility she may be at another location. But we do know that Brayden is involved. This isn't a coincidence. I need to get in that house and physically search for Ciera myself before we confront Brayden." I answered.

"Well damn..." Nathan sighed. "This ain't gone work. Ciera is family. So that means I'll still owe Leon." Nathan turns his gaze to Trust and Loyal. "Let's get to work," Nathan said.

Loyal and Trust got up and grabbed three cases of different sizes. They each opened a case, cleaned their weapons, and loaded the guns with ammo. To say I was shocked at learning this new side of Loyal was an understatement, but then again, everyone has a secret.

"So..." Nathan said, "Here's the plan...."

☐

CHAPTER 22

Glen

As I sat in my home office, the sound of Le Andria Johnson's 'Better Days' filled the air, resonating through the speakers throughout my house. I was captivated by the lyrics. The song was speaking directly to my soul. As I gazed out the window, I couldn't help but notice the gloomy overcast mirrored the turmoil I felt within. I have never, in my life, felt as lost as I do right now. I feel like I failed at being a husband, father, and brother. I have no clear direction on what my next step is going to be.

I threw my empty beer bottle in the trash beside my desk and went to the kitchen to grab another bottle from the fridge. I listened to the song's words as I walked through the empty house. Sherry had left with Brenda to help repaint her walls since the bullet holes and windows had already been replaced and repaired.

I grabbed the beer and closed the fridge. I was just heading back to my office when the doorbell rang. Turning directions, I went to the door and checked the peephole. My brows furrowed together in shock when I realized it was Keon. He usually never comes over without calling first.

I opened the door. "Hey son, everything okay?"

"Hey Mr. Taylor."

"What I tell you about that. Call me Glen."

"Glen, you remember Nathan?" Keon pointed to Nathan.

"Yes I do, Loyal's dad," I said, holding my hand out. "How are you doing man?"

Nathan shook my hand in return. "I'm good. How are you holding up?"

"By the grace of God. Yall come on inside." I said, holding the door open wider for them. "Sherry's not here. She went with Brenda to help paint the house."

"That's a great idea," Nathan said, looking at Keon before pulling out his phone and making a call.

"What's going on?" I questioned with a confused look.

"Do you have a place we can sit and talk?" Keon asked.

"Yeah, follow me," I said, leading both to my office. Nathen was still talking on the phone. "...yeah, Loyal, call Brielle, tell her to go to her mom's house and help her and her aunt paint.... Alright."

Now, they had my attention. Why did they need Brielle with her mom? Is everything okay? I wondered. We entered my office, and I sat down behind my mahogany desk. I gestured for Keon and Nathan to take a seat. I turned the music off, silencing the whole house.

"So, what's this about?" I asked, my heart rate slowly rising.

Seeing him at my house unexpectedly with Keon told me this was serious. I had no idea what this impromptu meeting was about. I also knew I couldn't handle any more bad news.

Keon spoke up, "We have a lead,"

I held my breath, afraid that I misheard him. "You have a lead," I repeated. Keon nodded his hand. "What lead?" I asked.

"We have the VIN number to the Dodge Durango involved in the kidnapping," Keon answered.

"What!" I shouted. "How?"

"Brielle is the one that got it," Keon answered.

"Brielle? How…w-when? Why didn't she tell me?"

"That's something you should speak to her about. I can tell you that I ran into her right after she got it. When she told me what happened, I took the VIN number from her and told her not to tell anyone."

"What the hell, Keon!" I yelled. "What gives you the right-"

"Mr. G!" Keon yelled, cutting me off. "Listen to me! Time is of the essence. My dad works for the government."

I knew what his dad did for a living and that Nathan was an assassin. A highly sought-after killer. He had a 100 percent success rate. Thanks to the background check I did a while back; I knew Leon and Nathen were dangerous men.

"I gave the VIN number to my dad, and he reported back to me with some information following his investigation. We know who the car was registered to." Keon finished.

"Who?" I asked.

"Brayden Reed

Are my ears deceiving me? "Brayden Reed… my employee, Brayden?" Keon nodded his head. "I'll kill him!" I growled as I jumped up from my seat and walked towards the door.

Keon was standing in front of the door before I could reach the knob with his arms folded across his chest. Keon had an inch on me and was built, but that meant nothing to me.

"Boy, if you don't get out of my way!" I yelled.

"I will, but you need to hear me out first, have a seat." He said, gesturing to the chair behind my desk.

"I heard enough!" I shouted.

"I have a lead on where Ciera might be held," Keon stated.

I glared at him as he gestured for me to take a seat. I took a deep breath as I returned to my chair. I watched as Nathan sat calmly in his chair. Not a tensed muscle in his body. The look in his eyes told me he wasn't worried, but I knew he was worried about Ciera. She'd spent just as much time with his girls as Brielle did.

"My dad also gave me the address to his newest property. He believes Ciera is being held there."

"Then why the fuck are we sitting here? Let's go!" I said, getting frustrated.

"I already have some men on the way there," Nathan finally spoke up.

"You have men? And just what is it that you do, Nathan?" I asked.

"You know exactly what it is that I do. I allowed the background check."

I nodded, "You allowed?"

"Just so happens, we both have the same connection."

"I didn't know you worked with others," I stated.

"I don't. I'm training. Now listen, as Keon stated. Time is of the essence. As you already know, I have no problem going in alone.

However, this situation is delicate. It's obvious that this is personal for Brayden."

"Oh, you bet your ass it's personal," I said. Nathan gave me a nod.

"In that case, keep him away from the house. That way, he keeps his life... or at least until you're done with him."

I immediately picked up my phone and dialed Mike. I put the call on speaker while waiting for him to pick up.

"What's good?" Mike greeted me.

"Mike, are you at the office?" I asked.

"Yeah, what's up? You need something?"

"Is Brayden at the office?"

"Yeah, I saw that fool around. I just talked with his ass yesterday about hanging out at the office."

"Keep his ass there. His ass kidnapped Ciera... and Mike, don't let him know we know. I'm on my way."

"You got it, boss." He said before hanging up.

Nathan got up and nudged Keon. "Let's roll, kid."

"Alright. Glen, I'll text you with an update." Keon said.

I nodded as I grabbed my keys from the desk. I followed them out and locked the door before heading to the office.

When I arrived, I went straight to my office. After finding it empty, I made my way to Mike's office. I heard Mike speaking to Brayden before I opened the door. "...has to be in Arizona."

I walked into the office with all eyes on me. "Hey, boss," Mike said.

"Aye Glen... How are you doing?" Brayden smiled.

It took everything in me not to bust him in his mouth. Instead, I inhaled deeply. "As good as I can be. What's going on in here?" I asked, grabbing a chair and sitting in front of the door, blocking it.

"Nothing much. Just talking to Brayden about work. He's still unsure about choosing a client. Do you think you might want to take a leave of absence?" Mike asked Brayden.

"That actually doesn't sound like a bad idea," Brayden responded.

"You're willing to give up pay for your girlfriend? How would she feel about that." I asked.

"Oh, I don't think she'll mind. She hates being at the house alone. To be honest, I'm thinking about relocating to another state." Brayden answered.

"Oh really! Why don't you tell me about her?" I asked, leaning forward in my seat.

The moment he started talking, I peeked at my cell. Keon needed to hurry up. My patience was running thin. My part in this just started, and I don't know how much more of this I can take.

☐

CHAPTER 23

Keon

We arrive at the one-story house one hour after leaving Glen's house. This was the longest hour of my life. The whole time, I prayed that Ciera was at this address. If not, I had no idea where to look. I knew Brayden was behind this, and knowing his selfish ass, he'll take her whereabouts to the grave. When Nathan turned the car off, I reached for the door.

"Wait a minute, son. Before we go in here, there are some rules you must follow." Nathan's serious tone made me pause, my hand still on the door handle.

"Okay," I said, giving him my full attention.

"As much as you might want to go in here screaming Ciera's name, don't. Remain professional and don't touch anything. Keep in mind this is my job. You are only here for Ciera. Lastly, trust your instincts. Let me know immediately if something doesn't feel right or you sense danger. Do you understand my rules?"

"Yes Sir," I said.

"Good, let's go get your girl."

Loyal and Trust exited their silver Dodge Charger when we stepped out of the car. I was surprised to see they both had changed clothes and were wearing Gray suits with black button-up shirts. I thought it weird that Nathan had changed before leaving the yacht. We'd left before Loyal and Trust.

We walked up to the house looking like salespeople. Which was cool because it was still daylight. The last thing we needed was to draw attention from the neighbors. Once we were at the door, Loyal discreetly picked the lock.

"There's a camera. Is it taken care of?" Nathan asked.

"Already disabled, Pops," Trust said as Loyal unlocked the door.

Once inside and the door was closed, Nathan and Trust immediately drew their guns. Loyal had a video recorder in his hand, but I could see the butt of the gun strapped to his hip.

Trust stood at the entrance, holding his gun tightly. With caution, Nathan guided Loyal and me towards the first door to our left. Which happened to lead us into the garage. Inside, a black Dodge Durango caught our attention. Nathan kept a watchful eye while Loyal meticulously documented the car's exterior with his video camera. He made sure to capture the vehicle's details, including the paper license plates and the vehicle registration, showing Brayden as the owner.

The stillness of the house echoed our footsteps as we moved from one room to another. We walked through the house, exploring each room. Each room was empty except for the master bedroom and the living room. After searching the whole house, we met Trust in the living room.

"Are you sure this is the right address?" Loyal asks me.

"Yeah. It must be that's the Durango in the garage. This makes no sense. She has to be here." I said frustrated.

"Loyal, Trust, go check the backyard," Nathan commanded. They nodded before turning towards the kitchen to go out the back door. "Did Leon give you the address to the other properties that Brayden is affiliated with?" He asked me.

"No. My dad did his own investigation. He said she would be here. This is the only place he would come and go from."

"Unless he's working with someone else. Ciera could be with the accomplice."

I shrugged, "If that's the case, we're right back where we started, with no lead."

"Oh... we have a lead," Nathan smirked.

"Brayden won't talk," I said.

"I'm not worried about that. If Brayden knows where Ciera is, I can get it out of him."

I was at a loss for words. I felt like I let Ciera, Glen, and Brielle down. The back door closing snapped me out of my pity party. "Pops, did you check behind every door?" Trust asked.

"Yeah, why?" Nathan answered.

"We missed something. This house has a basement." Loyal said.

"Are you sure? Houses over here don't have basements." Nathan said.

"This is a new development. He could have paid extra to have one put in." I said.

"Well... from the looks of it, he did," Trust said after opening a closet door. "There's a basement window outback. He tried to cover it with the tarp." He said as he dragged his hand against the wall of the closet.

I started opening doors and checking walls as well. I went into the kitchen and opened a door that led to a pantry. I started moving shelving and boxes from the wall until I came to another door that had a padlock. "Nathan! I found something!" I shouted.

I moved out of the pantry as Nathan went in, followed by Loyal with the camcorder. "Trust, bolt cutters," Nathan said.

Trust steps forward, cutting the bolt lock off the door. He and Nathan headed down the dark stairwell, followed by Loyal and me. Loyal continued to videotape their every move.

Once at the bottom of the stairs, someone flipped the light switch, showing an empty room with a cement floor. The air was hot and stuffy. One door was connected to the room with a bolt lock on it. Trust cut the lock, and Nathan went in, followed by Trust, both with their guns drawn. The moment the door was opened, I was hit with a God-awful smell of urine, vomit, and blood.

"Loyal, get in here!" Nathan yelled. "Hurry up, get as much as you can." Loyal took off in a hurry, with me following behind him."

"Ciera!" I yelled as I ran to her.

Her arms were bound by shackles, and she was naked. Despite my calling out to her, she remained motionless. I gently turned her head to face me. What I saw was a sight that sent chills down my spine. Her face was covered in blood, and her eye was swollen shut.

"Cut her free!" I yelled as I noticed the bloodstains on the wall. "Ciera! Baby, open your eyes", I said, gently shaking her. When she didn't respond, I checked for a pulse. "She doesn't have a pulse!" I yelled as I laid her flat on the floor and started doing compressions.

"One, two, three, four…" I cringed when I felt her rib crack. Loyal gave Trust the camcorder, and he continued taping as Loyal positioned himself at Ciera's head. "…twenty-eight, twenty-nine, thirty," I said, watching as Loyal lifted her chin upward and gave her two rescue breaths.

We did three cycles before I checked for a pulse. "She has a pulse, but it's faint," I said, relieved.

"Grab her, let's go," Nathan said.

I picked her up bridal style, and Loyal covered her with the sheet before we ran out of the house. I was surprised at how light she was.

"Trust, Nova is already in position. Get that video to her now! Loyal, you ride with me and Keon." Nathan shouted out as we rushed out.

"I'll text you when it's done." Trust yelled before opening the door to his car.

Loyal opened the back door, and I slid inside with Ciera lying on my lap.

"Ciera, I got you, baby, stay with me…"

☐

CHAPTER 24

Glen

"Naw man, I ain't try'in to hear your excuses. That's a punk move." Mike said to Brayden.

"Don't you agree, Glen?" Mike asked, giving me eye contact.

"Hell yeah… it just shows how much of a coward you are," I responded. "Take Mike, for instance. He came into this company, letting Gerald and I know what he expected from this business and his plans. He made shit happen by his actions, which is how he is moving up in the company," I said.

Brayden's cell phone rang. I could see Levi calling from where I was sitting on the side. Play your role, Glen. I kept telling myself. Once Brayden declined the call, I continued. "You are sitting here telling us what you expect from us, but you can't even take a client. Then you tell us You've been sneaking around with this girl for a year, and her family doesn't know about you."

"She seems pretty young," Mike said.

Brayden nods, "She's in her early 20s."

I looked down at the phone in my hand. We've been talking to this punk for over an hour now, and still no update. I know Brayden's talking about Ciera, and I don't know exactly how much more of this I can take. "See what you don't understand, Brayden, that every choice you make has a consequence, whether good or bad." A text alert interrupts me. Both Brayden and I look at our phones.

Keon: We got her. Graceland Memorial Hospital NOW!

I looked up at Brayden just as he finished reading his text.

"Shit," he whispered.

We both stood simultaneously, and I stepped to him, giving him an uppercut that lifted him off his feet. He came down, hitting his head on the corner of the table against the wall, knocking him out cold.

"What's the word?" Mike asked, still sitting behind his desk.

"They found Ciera. She's on the way to Graceland Memorial."

"Damn, way out there! I'm rolling with you. I'll drive." Mike insisted as he stood up.

"Let's tie this jackass up first. Then I'm going to shut this place down. I got some zip ties in my office." I said as I ran out the door. I stopped by the receptionist's desk on the way to my office. "Kim, clear out the building. I want this office closed in 2 minutes. You get the rest of the day off with pay."

"Okay." She responded as she got up in a hurry. I'm sure she heard the urgency in my voice.

I continued to my office, grabbed a handful of zip ties from my desk drawer and hurried back to Mike's office.

"Here, use these to hogtie his ass," I said, handing him the ties.

"You don't want to use cuffs?"

"No, his punk ass knows how to get out of them. I'm about to help Kim clear the building." I said as I rushed out of the room. Five minutes later, I was locking up and hopped in the car with Mike. "Shit, Did you get his phone?" I asked.

"Yeah," he said, pulling it out of his back pocket and handing it to me. I put it in the glove compartment."

"That nigga Levi called him earlier. Im'ma have his ass too, if I find out he has something to do with this." I pulled out my cell and called Sherry. She answered after the first ring.

"Hello"

"Baby, are you still at Brenda's?"

"Yeah, Brielle is here too. What's going on? You sound panicky."

"They found Ciera!"

"Oh my god! They found her?" She screamed.

"Yeah. Meet me at Graceland Memorial."

"We're on our way... They found my baby. We gotta-" I heard her scream before she disconnected the line.

I checked my phone for more updates from Keon. There were no further updates. Why didn't he tell me she was okay? I glanced at the last message he sent. '

Keon: We got her. Graceland Memorial Hospital NOW!

Staring at that message again sent chills down my spine. What's wrong with Ciera?

☐

CHAPTER 25

Keon

"Any updates for Ciera Taylor?" I asked the nurse at the nurses' station. She looked at me with irritation.

"Not since five minutes ago. Like I said, sir. We're still running tests. The doctor will be out to update you as soon as he knows something."

"Son, come sit with us for a moment," Nathan said, touching my shoulder. He looked at the nurse. "I'm sorry." She gave him a soft smile before typing away at the computer. With a hand on my shoulder, Nathan guided me to a row of chairs against the back wall of the waiting room. "I know you worried, son, we all are." He pointed to himself and Loyal. "We gotta stay positive. Let's consider no news as good news, okay?"

"They should know something by now. We've been here for two hours," I exasperated, taking a seat next to Loyal. I looked at him and did a double take when I noticed he was wearing the same black joggers and red t-shirt he had this morning at the yacht. Nathan saw the look on my face.

"As you may know, our profession is top secret." He warned. I gave him a nod. "If anyone asks, you and Loyal were together. I met you guys here. Understand?" I gave him another nod.

"…Excuse me, we're looking for Ciera Taylor." I looked up at the sound of her voice.

"And you are?" The nurse questioned.

"Mrs. Taylor!" I called out as I hopped up and walked towards her.

"Keon! Oh my God!" She said as she hurried to me, pulling me into an embrace. Loyal and Nathan walked towards Brenda and Brielle to comfort them. They were crying both happy and worried tears. "Do you know what happened? Who found her?" Sherry sobbed.

"Have you seen her yet?" Brenda asked.

"Any updates?" Asked Brielle.

"No, we haven't been updated as of yet," Nathan answered.

"Oh, Nathan!" Sherry hugged him, noticing he was here for the first time. "Thank you so much for coming."

"You don't have to thank me, we're family." He replied.

Sherry looked around, "Is Glen here?"

"Not yet. He should be here any minute." I said, and no later than I responded to Sherry, we heard his voice screaming her name.

"Sherry!" Glen shouted as he took quick strides to where we stood. Mike followed close behind him. Sherry held her arms open as he stepped into her embrace.

"You okay babe?" He asked, kissing her forehead.

"Yeah, but what of Ciera? What's wrong with her? Why are we here?" She cried. Glen turned his attention to me.

"Keon… what happened?" He asked.

All eyes settled on me as I began to recount the horrifying discovery we made. "When we found Ciera, she was naked and shackled to the wall." An audible gasp escaped from each person's lips. Tears welled up in their eyes as the gravity of the situation sunk in. Glen's face turned rigid, his expression reflecting a mix of shock and anger. "She was beaten pretty badly," I muttered. "Her right eye was swollen shut, and she had a nasty gash on the side of her forehead." I took a deep breath. The thought of my next words brought tears to my own eyes. "She had no pulse when we found her."

"Oh my God, No!" Sherry cried.

"No!" Brielle yelled as she fell to her knees. Loyal was holding her up.

"She's okay babe." Loyal whispered to Brielle

"Damn," Mike yelled, his body tense as if he wanted to hit something.

Glen started shaking as he held Sherry. Nathan comforted Brenda as she cried out. I continued, "Loyal and I performed CPR until we got a pulse, but it was weak."

"Listen, everyone. I was told Ciera still had a pulse when she arrived over an hour ago. The doctors haven't been out yet, so let's take no news as good news, alright?" Nathan said, still comforting Brenda. "Here," Nathan gestured towards the chairs. "Everyone, have a seat. I'll go and see if we can get an update." He said as he walked Brenda to the chair. I sat down, praying for an update as Nathan went to the nurses' station.

"For Taylor!..." An older man shouted, wearing light blue scrubs.

"That's us!... Over here!" Everyone said, jumping to their feet.

The doctor made his way towards us. "Family for Ciera Taylor?" he confirmed.

"Yes, how is she?" Glen answered.

"My name is Doctor Smitz. First and foremost,... Ciera is alive." There was a sigh of relief from every person in our group.

"Thank you God!" Sherry said.

"However," The doctor continued. "She has been through a lot. I'm guessing she was held captive?"

"Yes, she was missing and was just rescued," Glen answered.

The doctor nodded his head. "She has skin breakdown on both wrists and ankles. They are infected, and she has been given antibiotics to combat the infection. She also has rhabdomyolysis, which is muscle breakdown. This, on its own, can be life-threatening if not treated in time. She's currently being given fluids and electrolytes through I.V."

"How's her kidneys?" Sherry asked.

"Her kidneys are fine. It looks like we caught this at the beginning stage." Sherry nodded her head as the doctor continued. "She also has a few fractured ribs. To my understanding, she was given CPR before being brought in?"

"Yes," Loyal and I answered together.

"Fractured ribs can sometimes occur during CPR. However, there were also broken ribs in the advanced stages of healing. Furthermore, Ciera also has a fractured skull. Specifically, it is a hairline fracture, meaning there is a small crack in the bone. A deep gash on the side of her forehead required stitches. Ciera is severely dehydrated. The blood test also revealed that she is malnourished and anemic. Lastly, Ciera's HCG levels are elevated."

Sherry gasped, bringing her hands to her mouth. "HCG levels!"

"What does that mean??" I asked.

"It means Ciera's pregnant." Doctor Smitz said.

"Pregnant!" Glen and I shouted. Glen grabbed my shoulder. "Please tell me it's your baby." I shook my head slightly.

"Where do her levels put her?" Brenda asked.

"Uh… I would say about three or four weeks. We would have to talk to Ciera about her last menstrual cycle." The doctor said.

"Can't you just do an ultrasound?" Glen asked.

Doctor Smitz shook his head. "Not at this time. It's too soon. It would be too small to see on the screen and too soon to hear a heartbeat."

Glen's body tensed up as he went back to sit on the chair. Tears fell from his eyes as he repeatedly punched the side of his head. Nathan went over to him, taking a seat next to him. I couldn't hear what was being said.

"When can we see her?" Brielle asked.

"We are admitting her. She's being transferred to another room as we speak. She is sedated, so don't be alarmed by her unconscious state. She will be in room 5227. Three visitors at a time."

"Thank you," we all said in unison before racing towards the hospital room from the ER.

Sherry, Glen, and I walked into Ciera's room. I never thought in a million years that I would see my future in such a tragic state, lying in a hospital bed with a swollen-shut black eye. Her head was wrapped in gauze, and her wrists were also bandaged. Her ankles were hidden from view under the sheet. She wore a hospital gown that seemed to highlight the fragility of her bruised body. Her one good eye appears sunken in. Her beautiful hair was stiff, dull, and dry. Her two French braids were grown out.

Sherry cried as she ran over to her side and held her hand. Glen did the same to the opposite side. "Oh baby! Mommy's here." She cried.

"Daddy, too," Glen said as he kissed her cheek. "You're safe now baby. You just rest up and heal."

My silent tears turned into audible sobs as my body trembled uncontrollably. The overwhelming waves of anger washed over me as I stared at Ciera lying in that bed. I felt myself losing control. He dared to touch her… he laid his fuckin hands on her and forced himself on her. The thought echoed in my mind.

"I'm going to kill him! Where is he?" I muttered fiercely; my teeth clenched in rage.

Glen walked over to me at that moment, pulling me into a stiff embrace. "No, you're not. That's my job. He will be dealt with. I promise you that. You hear me?" he spoke directly into my ear. His voice was threatening and seeping with anger.

"Huh… you guys know who did this?" she asked from the side of Ciera's bed. Glen turned towards her and nodded.

"Brayden," I scuffed.

"Brayden… Why does that name sound familiar?" she asked.

I walked over, taking a seat next to Ciera's bed. I took her hand and pressed it against my lips. My eyes landed on her stomach, causing more tears to spill.

He worked for me." Glen answered Sherry as he walked over to her, pulling her into a hug.

"Why would he do this?" She cried.

"I don't know babe," Glen said.

"Are you going to let him get away with this?" she asked.

Glen stared at Ciera. His jaw locked in anger. He quickly kissed Sherry on the forehead. "I'll be back. You and Keon stay with Ciera. I'll send the others up one by one."

Sherry nodded and gave him another hug. "I love you."

"Love you too babe." He responded before letting her go and heading out the door.

CHAPTER 26

Glen

I paced back and forth in the boxing ring in my office gym. I'm trying to be patient as Mike drags Brayden out of his office and onto a chair in the center of the ring. Nathan is standing just outside the ring with his arms crossed, staring at Brayden as if he was the scum on the bottom of his shoe.

"Aye! Watch it man, shit!" Brayden snapped.

"Shut your ass up!" Mike yelled while shoving him onto the chair. "You want me to untie his ass?" Mike asked.

I thought about it briefly, wondering if I should let Brayden give me a challenge, but thought against it. "Hell no! Keep his ass locked up like he did my daughter."

"Hahaha… so that's what this is about. You found Ciera!" Brayden laughed while Mike tied his ankles to the leg of the chair and his hands behind his back.

Mike punched Brayden in the mouth, busting his lip. "You think this is funny? We'll see who has the last laugh." Mike growled.

Brayden spit out blood and a tooth and smiled. His teeth were stained red with blood.

The smile is what did it for me. Without a second thought, I made my way towards him and unleashed a series of vigorous punches, repeatedly striking his face and landing a final blow to his stomach before backing away from him.

Brayden's grunts turned into laughs, "Is that all you got?" he taunted.

"Hell no! Mike, cut his ass loose." I shouted.

After Mike cut Brayden loose, Brayden jumped to his feet and stalked toward me. He threw a right and left hook, his fists aiming to land a blow. However, I quickly reacted and blocked both of his hits with precision. Not wasting any time, I retaliated by swiftly giving him a powerful foot to the chest. He stumbled backward, regained his balance, and charged at me. I threw my arms around his neck and delivered a knee strike to his chest, knocking the wind out of him. Releasing my grip, I swiftly sent my elbow crashing into his nose, breaking it. The pain was evident on his face as blood began to flow from his broken nose.

"You ready to talk now? Who was working with you? Because I know you didn't pull this shit off alone." I quizzed as I watched him stumble back to me, covered in blood.

"Fuck you! I ain't tell'in your ass shit!" He said, spitting out blood.

"Yes, you are," Nathan added calmly as he opened a black case on the table just outside the boxing ring. He turned the case around, showing different tools used to torture someone. "The way I see it, you can tell us voluntarily or involuntarily."

"Who the fuck are you?" Brayden sneered.

"Who I am is none of your concern. Now… who was your accomplice?" Nathan asked.

"Get the fuck outta here, I ain't telling you shit. This doesn't concern you!" Brayden shouted as he turned his gaze back to me and got in a fighting stance.

"Wrong answer," Nathan said. Without looking, he quickly grabbed what looked like a nail gun out of his case and shot it at Brayden, making him drop to the floor as he screamed out.

"Argh! Shit man, What the hell." Brayden screamed, rocking back and forth on the floor. I could see the end of the silver nail embedded in his knee.

"You want to tell us who's working with you, or shall we test out more of my tools?" Nathan asked as he inspected his nail gun.

"Yo… I'm going through this nigga's text messages. From the looks of it, Levi is his accomplice." Mike said from the corner of the ring.

I figured that motherfucker had something to do with it. I walked over to Brayden, who was still lying on the floor. I stepped on the knee with the nail embedded. "You had that piece of shit motherfucker plant false evidence on my brother!" I growled while getting down in his face.

"Argh!" He screamed out as he tried to push me off his knee.

"Who planted shit on me?"

My head snapped to the door, and confusion and relief filled me as I saw Gerald walking towards the ring. A woman sashayed in with him wearing a navy-blue skirt suit with black pumps. Her hair was straight with bangs. Her skin was the color of milk chocolate. Her movement screamed of confidence.

"Gerald! How are you here?" I asked.

Gerald looked at me and pointed to Nathan as he walked towards him. "Nathan, you are a fuckin life saver. Thanks, man." He said, giving Nathan a bro hug.

"You're good man. No need to thank me." Nathan turned to Glen and Mike. "This is my lawyer Nova." I gave her a quick nod.

"So, who planted that shit on me?" Gerald asked, getting back to the subject.

"From the looks of it, Levi did. The people that shot up your house were Levi's people," Mike said after reading more of Brayden's text messages.

"Send that nigga a message. Tell him to meet here and use the back door. His ass is going to get dealt with tonight." I said.

"Already did. Levi should be here in fifteen minutes." Mike said.

"Are there any security cameras on the premises?" Nova asked.

"Yeah, good lookin' out. I'll disable them," Mike said, jumping out of the ring.

"I'll come with you." Nova insisted, following behind Mike as he walked out of the gym.

"My family was in that house, you son of a bitch!" Gerald yelled at Brayden.

"That was the fuckin point..." Brayden said just before I backhanded him in the mouth, interrupting him.

"Who is this Levi character?" Nathan asked.

"A dirty ass cop," Gerald answered.

Nathan checked the watch on his wrist. "It's nothing I hate more than a dirty cop."

"What the hell you got against my family?" Gerald asked.

Brayden was still sitting on the floor, leaning back against the ring. He was no longer rocking back and forth, but I could tell he was still in pain. He was sweating, and his breathing was erratic. "I don't have anything against your family. My problem is with you."

Gerald calmly pulled up a chair and sat down. "What the hell did I do to you to make you go after my family."

"You killed my brother! He was the only family I had left, and I wanted you to see how it felt to have someone you loved taken away from you." Brayden yelled.

Gerald and I shared a look before he asked the next question. "Who was your brother?"

"Mason Reed!" Brayden shouted.

"Mason!" Gerald and I said in unison.

"The same Mason that broke into my house and tried to kill my daughter?" Gerald asked.

"Mason's ass deserved to die. His ass not only put his hands on my niece, but he almost killed Brenda," I said.

Nathan stood with both arms crossed, one hand massaging his chin. "So… if you are upset with Gerald for killing your brother. Why go after Ciera? You're going after both men when you have quarrel with only one."

"Because Gerald was also Mason's father, and I'm sure Glen knew that shit too. Yall rich motherfuckers turned your back on family. We grew up poor and shit, and yall livin' the damn life."

"Damn, bro!" I looked at Gerald, who had a confused look on his face. "Gerald, is that true? Did you have another child?" I asked.

"Hell no! Brielle is my only kid." Gerald turned his gaze back to Brayden. "What the hell would make you think I was Mason's father?"

"Because you raped my mom!" Brayden shouted.

"Get the fuck outta here, I ain't never raped nobody! What the hell are you talking about? What's your mother's name?"

"Tilly," Braydon sneered.

"Tilly! Tilly Pierson! Big booty Tilly with that big ass birthmark on her neck?" I asked.

"Watch how you speak of my mom bitch-ass..." Brayden said, sizing me up.

"Or what?" I asked, interrupting him. "Shut your dumb ass up before I have Nathan put another nail in your kneecap," I said, looking down at him.

"So, you're that Brayden," Gerald said, as if he's finally realizing who he's talking to. "I hate to tell you this Brayden, but your mama was a hoe." Gerald laughed.

I laughed with him because I knew the story Gerald was about to tell. Brayden was about to get a rude awakening.

"Fuck you!" Brayden said through clenched teeth.

"She did!" Gerald laughed. "As well as everyone else. "I was with your mother for two years before I caught her stepping out on me. She cheated on me with your dad. I hate to break it to you son, but your daddy may not be your daddy."

Brayden remained quiet as he listened to Gerald."

Gerald continued, "It's a good chance I might be your daddy. But most importantly, I didn't rape your mother. I doubt if she even was raped. That could have been an excuse she told your father to explain her unexpected pregnancy. However, there is absolutely no chance that I could have fathered Mason. That means this anger.. this vendetta that you have against me and mine, it should have been towards your mother. She's the one that fucked up your life." Gerald said, getting up.

Suddenly, the back door opened, and Levi walked in. His eyes widened when he laid eyes on us inside the ring. Before he could reach for his gun, Nathan gave him a single shot to the head.

"How much I owe you?" I asked Nathan, I wasn't expecting him to kill Levi, but I wasn't complaining. What's done is done."

"I usually charge 95k but for crooked cops, since I hate them the most, I charge less. But since your family, it's on the house." He said, putting his gun in his back holster.

"So, if you're not Mason's father, then why did she mention your name as her rapist?" Brayden asked, not caring that Levi was just gunned down.

"Your mother wasn't the brightest in the bunch. I hadn't seen that woman since the day I put her ass out, around the time you were conceived. I have no idea why her dumb ass did what she did."

"You talking all this shit about my mom, and she ain't here to defend herself." Brayden said.

"Well… last I heard she passed away. You'll be able to speak to her soon enough because you're not leaving this building with air in your lungs." I said as I pulled my gun from my holster, putting a bullet in his chest and one in his head.

"Why don't you guys get to the hospital. I'll have this mess cleaned up. "Nathan said.

"I appreciate you, Nathan. Hey, could Nova get a paternity test done with a sample of his blood for me?

"Whoa! Wait a minute now. I don't give a damn if this punk is my blood. I don't need a paternity test." Gerald said.

"Unfortunately, you do. That motherfucker raped Ciera, and now she's pregnant." I said.

"Ciera's pregnant! You didn't think to tell me that shit when he was alive." Gerald yelled.

"I didn't want him to die knowing he possibly has a child on the way. I'm not sure what Ciera will decide to do about the pregnancy, but either way, I want to make sure this fool isn't Ciera's cousin."

Nathan gave me a nod. "Yeah, I'll make sure she takes a sample. Gerald, you'll have to give up your DNA as well. You two go ahead to the hospital. I'll get things cleaned up here." He said as he dialed a number in his phone. "Good evening Darius, I need the house special over at Diamond Watch Securities.... Yes..."

We heard, as Gerald and I rushed out of the building.

CHAPTER 27

Ciera

A dull throbbing pain pulsates relentlessly in my head. That's the first thing I felt in this darkness. Darkness... It's not as dark as it usually is. Why do I see flashes of light? I realize my eyes are closed when they start to open slowly. I shut them again, learning the light is too bright. It makes my headache worse. Where am I? This is not death... is it? I continue to lay with my eyes closed, taking in the quietness around me. I hear an occasional beeping sound, then the sliding of a chair. Who is grabbing my hand?

"Good morning, Ciera. I'm still here. Please try to wake up for me today. Okay, sweetheart. I need to see those beautiful eyes of yours."

I know that voice. "Mom?" I whisper in a broken voice as I softly squeeze her hand.

"Ciera, baby! Oh my God, you're awake. Open your eyes, baby." I could hear the smile in her voice.

"I can't. It's too bright."

"Hold on." She says, letting go of my hand. Moments later, I notice the brightness level fade behind my eyelid. "Okay, baby. I closed the curtain and turned the light off. Can you open your eyes now?" She asked, taking back my hand.

I slowly opened my eyes to a dimly lit room. My left eye barely opened, but I could still make out some things in front of me. My vision was a little cloudy. "Mom, where am I?"

"You're at the hospital, sweetheart. I've already paged your nurse. How are you feeling?" She asked, caressing my arm. I couldn't answer her. I was afraid to answer her. "Are you crying baby… Don't cry." She said as she gently wiped my tears. "The nurse will be here soon with pain meds, okay honey."

"Am I dreaming?" I asked with a broken voice. I didn't know if I could handle waking up if I was.

"No Ciera. You're not dreaming, baby." The door suddenly opens, and I jump out of fear and gasp in pain. It's okay… it's just your dad." My mom says, still rubbing my arm.

"She's awake?" My dad asks. I can hear the smile in his deep voice.

"Yeah. She just woke up. I already paged the nurse." My mom added.

"Why is it so dark in here." He asked.

"The brightness hurts her eyes." My mom answered.

"Hey baby girl."

"Hi Daddy."

Knock, knock … "Hello, somebody paged." The nurse said, coming into the room.

"Yes, my daughter is awake." My dad said.

"That's great news!" She says as she walks to the edge of the bed. "Hi Ciera, my name is Amber. How are you feeling? Any pain?"

I whispered, "Yes."

"Can you tell me where?"

"Everywhere," I responded.

"Okay, let me take your vitals and do a quick assessment before your doctor comes. Before we begin, I'll give you some pain meds through your I.V."

I gave her a slight nod.

By the time the nurse and doctor finished, I was beyond tired. I'd refuse to go to sleep. I feared sleep would take me back to where I was held captive. The questions that kept popping up in my head also contributed to my headache.

"Brayden took me," I stated. "He told me you believed I was dead and already had my funeral. Is that true?"

"No baby. We never once thought you were dead and never stopped looking for you." My mom said.

"That doesn't mean we weren't scared though. A lot of stuff happened while we were searching for you. Your bloody clothes and a weapon were found at Gerald's house. He was arrested for your disappearance."

I gasp. "No, Uncle Gerald had nothing to do with it. Is he still in jail?" I asked.

"No, sweetheart, he's back home now."

"Oh good." I sighed in relief. "How long was I gone for?"

"A month." My dad answered.

"Felt longer. How long have I been in the hospital?" I asked. The pain medicine was starting to kick in.

"Two days." My mom answered.

"What's wrong with me?" There was silence as my parents looked at each other as if trying to communicate silently about who would tell me. I felt my anxiety growing. Until now, they have been forthcoming about everything, but now they are hesitating. Was I dying? I broke the silence. "Okay, whatever it is, is it terminal?"

"No baby girl." My dad answered.

"Okay, so what's wrong with me?" I asked again.

"Well… When you were brought in, you were dehydrated and malnourished."

Okay, that's understandable, I thought to myself. I waited for my mom to continue, but she remained silent.

"Dehydration and malnourishment don't explain the bandages or the pain in my chest," I said.

"You have skin and muscle breakdown on your wrists and ankles as well as an infection. You're going to need physical therapy to get your strength back. You have a cracked skull and a deep gash on your forehead that required stitches. You have a black eye that is swollen shut. Thankfully, there are no broken bones or serious eyeball damage. It will heal." My mom said.

"Dang, cracked skull," I said in disbelief.

"Just a small one. There's one more thing." My mom said, grabbing my hand. My dad got up and started pacing the floor.

"What is it?" I asked, getting nervous again.

"Listen, baby, whatever you decide and whatever happens, we are here for you, okay?" My mom said.

"Okay," I answered nervously.

"You're pregnant, Ciera." She said.

"What! No, no, no, no…" I cried. "No, I can't be."

"Calm down, Ciera." My mom said.

"Calm down!" I yelled. The pain in my chest and head spiked.

My dad's phone chimed. He looked at his phone. "Keon is here, he's on his way up."

"No, I don't want to see him. Brayden said he moved on with someone else. He doesn't care about me. Send him away!" I yelled.

"What are you talking about baby girl? Keon Didn't move on. He was searching for you just like the rest of us." My mom said.

"Keon was the one that found you. He saved your life by giving you CPR. When you were found, you didn't have a pulse. That boy has not left her side since he found you. The only reason he's not here now is because I made him go home and freshen up." My dad walked over to me and grabbed my hand. "That man loves you, and because of him, you're lying here with us today. I'm not sending him away, and neither are you, you understand?" He asked. I nodded my head with silent tears sliding down my face.

"Does he know I'm pregnant?"

"Yes, he does, and he's still by your side. He's a good man Ciera."

A few minutes later, Keon enters the room with a bouquet already in a vase. He sat it down on the nightstand and greeted my parents before he noticed I was awake.

"Ciera, babe! You're awake," he smiled, kissing my cheek. I pulled away slightly, causing his small smile to fade. He grabbed my hand. "What's wrong? Are you in pain? You need the nurse?" I just closed my eyes and let the tears fall.

"It's alright, Keon. She just found out about the pregnancy. She needs time." I heard my mom say. I left my eyes closed and decided to let my tiredness take over.

It's been ten days since I was admitted to the hospital, and I finally received my discharge paper today. I've had daily visits from the physical therapist to help strengthen my muscles. Being shackled for a month and unable to stand or walk took a toll on me.

Keon walked in with a bag of my clothes. He helped me get dressed in black sweatpants and a white T-shirt. Although they were my clothes, I wasn't the size I once was, and the clothes just hung off my body. Keon has been by my side, constantly helping me get better. I was also diagnosed with PTSD and nyctophobia. I'm now afraid of the dark. My anxiety kicks in, and I feel I'm back in whatever room Brayden kept me in. I've been assigned to a therapist to talk to three times a week until I can handle things.

Keon pulled into the driveway of my house and helped me get out of the car. I wasn't surprised to see several cars parked on the street. I recognized most of them. Keon told me that I had guests waiting to welcome me home. The first thing I noticed when we walked through the door was the welcome home banner hanging on the wall in the living room. Second, the aroma of food hit me. I'm not sure what's cooking, but it had my mouth watering and my stomach growling.

"My favorite cousin is home!" Brielle yelled, approaching me and giving me a gentle hug before helping me into the living room.

I wasn't surprised to see all of Loyal's family there. As much time as I spent with Honor, Justice, and Lisa, I felt like an extended family member. I've grown to love each of them. Even Trust and his craziness. Nathan still scared me sometimes, but I loved him all the same.

Everyone started coming in one by one. "Chica, Oh my god, I missed you so much!" Jessica said as she kissed my cheek. "You let me know if it's anything you need okay." She turned to Keon. "Hey, butthead," she teased as she hugged him.

"Thanks for bringing back my friend." I heard her whisper before breaking their embrace.

My mother came out of nowhere, startling me as she whispered in my ear. "Baby, come with me. Let's get you something more fitting to wear."

"Yes, please," I responded. My clothes were too big, and my hair was dry and brittle like I got electrocuted. I've showered and washed my hair at the hospital, but their products did nothing for my skin or hair.

"Good, I can't have you over here lookin' a mess in front of all these people. This is not how you usually roll." My mom laughed. "Do you think you can walk up the stairs?"

"Yeah."

"Good, I'll help you. Come on."

Instead of going to my room, we detoured to the bathroom. I watched as she ran my water and helped me in. "Have you thought about what you will do about your pregnancy yet?"

"No," I sighed as I sank into the water.

She grabbed A washcloth and lathered it before bathing me. I could have washed myself, but I figured she needed this to soothe something within herself. She even washed my hair for me. Once I was dried off, she helped me oil my skin. I was shocked that my room was just the way I left it. There was a time when I thought I would never see this room again. On my bed was a white sweater and black leggings. Black boots were lying on the floor.

After I was dressed, my mom sat me at my vanity and did my hair. Instead of blow-drying, we condition it, leaving it curly and styling it in a pineapple bun. I put on a black scarf and made sure my edges were laid. After getting dressed, the last thing I did was put my earrings on, and I stared at myself in the mirror. I was actually starting to feel like myself again.

"Beautiful as always." She smiled as she stood behind me, looking at my reflection. I really love this sweater. It was small yet baggy, and it hung off of my shoulders.

"You ready to go down and mingle?" She asked.

"I guess so." I sighed. "Thanks for helping me."

"No problem honey." She hugged me.

We walked out of the room together, and when we got to the stairs, I was confused to see gold rose petals flowing down the stairs. We followed the trail down the steps and into the family room. The path led to a gold cut-out sign that said Marry Me. White and gold balloons were positioned around the sign. A chair sat off to the side.

"What's going on?" I asked as I noticed my family sitting silently around the living room. My mother gently pushed me towards the chair. "Who's this for?"

"It's for you," Keon said from the doorway. He had on black slacks and a black and gold button-up shirt. Keon slowly walked over to me with his hands in his pocket. When he approached me, he took both my hands into his.

"I have been walking around for months trying to find the perfect time and place to ask you this question, but no time or place was perfect enough. Once you were taken away from us, I realized that every time I was with you was the perfect time. The perfect place is any place that you are at with me. I've learned the hard way that I can't eat, sleep, or think without you by my side.

Ciera, if you would have me, I want to spend my days fulfilling your life with the joy and happiness you put into mine. I want to spend my days building a life and family with you."

Keon dropped to one knee and pulled a small black velvet box out of his pocket. He opened it, revealing a two-carat heart-shaped diamond ring. I gasped in between tears.

"Ciera Taylor, will you do me the honor of being my wife?"

I stood there, frozen. Tears continuously flow down my cheeks. I looked around the room, all eyes staring back at me. I turned my gaze back to Keon. "What about the pregnancy?" I asked.

"It doesn't matter what you decide, I'll support you. If you choose to keep the baby. I will love that baby as if it was my own."

I inhaled deeply, "In that case, yes. I will marry you." I cried.

He slid the ring on my finger as the room erupted in cheer. He stood up and kissed me passionately. I wrapped my arms around my man's neck feeling a surge of emotions as tears streamed down my cheeks. To say that I was surprised was an understatement. I had no idea Keon felt this way about me. As if saving my life wasn't enough, he just expressed his love for me in the most profound way possible. I loved this man with my heart and soul.

Breaking the kiss, Keon looked at me with a smile. "I told you I would make you Mrs. Wright one day." He laughed as we were bombarded with people rushing up congratulating us with hugs and kisses.

Hours went by as we ate, laughed, danced, and celebrated. Well... they danced, I watched. I was still recovering, so I couldn't move around too much. Ding dong...

"I'll get it!" my mom said as she rushed to the door. Moments later, she returned, followed by a woman dressed in a jean jumpsuit with a white belt around her waist. "Keon," Mom said with a look of confusion. "This woman is here for you."

Keon took one look at her and stood up angrily. "What the hell are you doing here, Leilani?"

She smiled as she stepped to Keon and rubbed his cheek. "I missed you."

Keon slapped her hand away. "Keep your hands off me. How did you find me?" he growled.

"What the hell is going on here?" Uncle Glen asked.

Leilani smacked her lips, "How do you think? Now stop playing. Are you going to introduce me to everyone? Is Jessica here?" she asked, looking around.

Jessica emerged from the hallway at the mention of her name. Coming from that direction, she must have gone to the bathroom. Her eyes grew wide when she saw Leilani standing near her brother. She walked straight towards her.

"Bitch!" she yelled as she grabbed her by her hair and dragged her to the doorway. "I told your ass to stay away from my family!" she yelled as she threw her against the front door. She repeatedly punched her in the face as she yelled, "You want to say my name now bitch!"

Loyal and my dad rushed to pull Jessica off of Leilani, but somehow, she got free and ran back to Leilani, who was struggling to get off the floor. Jessica started stomping her.

"Stalking ass bitch, stay away from my brother!" Jessica yelled before they attempted to pull her away again.

Everyone was so engrossed in the commotion that no one noticed the moment I snuck away. I walked back down the stairs carefully with my gun in my hand. When I approached Jessica and Leilani. Leilani had the upper hand while everyone was holding back Jessica. It seemed as if nobody wanted to touch Leilani. I casually walked over to Leilani and grabbed her by her messed-up weave. With all the strength I could muster, I threw her against the door, and she slid to the floor. I hit her in the face with the butt of the gun and pulled her to her knees with the gun barrel aimed at her temple. Click, the sound of me pulling back the safety got everyone's attention. Even Leilani's.

"Ciera, don't!" My dad yelled.

I saw Keon approach me from the side. Instead of stopping me, he took his place next to me. I knew Keon could hold his own, but I was his woman, and it was about time Leilani got that through her fat-ass head. I ignored everyone, as well as the pain in my chest. I ignored the pleading of my family telling me to calm down.

"Listen here bitch! Keon is my man, now and forever. If I catch you creepin' around him, me, or popping up at my home again. I have a bullet in the chamber with your name on it. Do you understand where the fuck I'm coming from bitch? If not, try me!" I sneered.

Keon brought me into his arms and kissed the side of my face. He carefully takes the gun from my hands, puts the safety on, and hands the gun to my dad. Leilani's face is bloodied, but that doesn't stop her ugly face from frowning when Keon kisses me.

"Get your ass out of my house!" My mom yelled.

Leilani eyed me up and down as she got up. Before she could turn her head to leave, I punched her in the face and hid the pain that flared in my wrist.

"Calm down, babe. Not only did you just get out of the hospital, but you're pregnant." Keon reminded me. I watched as Leilani stumbled out of the house. My mother slammed the door behind her.

Everyone returned to the living room, getting comfortable once again. Jessica was still heated but calming down with the help of Brielle, Honor, and Justice.

"So, anyone want to tell us what the hell that was about?" Trust asked, looking between Keon, Jessica, and I.

Everyone remained quiet as they all had the same question. Jessica and Keon told them the story about Leilani being Keon's ex and how she cheated on him with their father and has been stalking Keon.

"Damn man, that girl is crazy as hell! I can't believe she slept with your pops the moment he came to visit. What a great way to say welcome home!" Trust laughed in disbelief. "Didn't he know that was your girl?" he asked.

"No, but Leilani knew he was my father. She'd seen pictures of him before pursuing him." Keon said.

"I can't believe I let her in my house. I should've had her nasty ass wait outside." My mom said. "Even though I don't condone fighting in my house, Jessica I'm glad you took it to the entryway without tearing up my house." She added.

"Okay, now I have a question," Loyal stated. He turned his attention to Brielle sitting on a stool across from him. "Babe, you want to explain how you got the VIN number to Brayden's car?" Brielle and her mom just stared at each other.

"Brie… you found the VIN number! How? I didn't see you the day I was kidnapped." I asked, "Believe me, I was searching for anyone to help me.."

Brenda walked over, stood by Brielle, and took her hand as she looked around. "Okay, well… We are all family here," she shrugged. "What if I told you all that this was not our reality two years ago today."

"Okay, babe, what you got in your cup?" Gerald laughed.

"Whatever it is, I need some of that!" Lisa said, looking at her cup.

Nathan kissed her on the cheek. "I know what I need." He tried to whisper in her ear but failed.

"Ugh, Daddy!" Honor and Justice whined, causing everyone to laugh.

After everyone quieted down and listened to Brenda and Brielle tell their story about being able to delve into the past. Everyone was left speechless. Especially me. I was thankful for their gift; I would be dead right now if it wasn't for Brielle.

Loyal was at a loss for words when he found out it was hereditary, with only women having the talent.

"Okay, okay," My dad shouted. "This day has gone from a welcome home party to an engagement party, a boxing match, and now a family confession." He laughed. "Are we adjourned, or does anyone else have something to say?"

I raised my hand. "I have two things to say."

"Go ahead baby girl." My dad said.

"I decided to drop out of school and work full time with you and Uncle Gerald."

"Are you sure, Ciera?" My dad asked.

"Yes, I can't ever see myself going back to that campus or any other for that matter."

My dad nodded as he looked at me and Uncle Gerald. Uncle Gerald gave him a nod. "Alright, on one condition. You continue talking to your therapist and do whatever they ask of you."

"Yeah, 'cause that shit you pulled earlier can't happen again." Uncle Gerald added.

"Never pull out a gun unless you intend on using it," Nathan said. Uncle Gerald and my dad nodded their head in agreement.

"I get what y'all are saying. I normally use my fist to get my point across, but my body is currently under construction. It didn't look like Leilani understood a beat down anyway because Jessica had already gave her one."

"Hell yeah, I did." She interrupted.

"...so I guess using my gun spoke to her in her language."

"God, I missed you!" Jessica laughed, giving her a fist bump.

"Ugh... I don't know what I'm going to do with you two," Lisa said, shaking her head.

"So, you said you had two things. What else did you want to say?" my mom asked.

I looked at my whole family before my eyes landed on Keon. "I decided to keep the baby."

"Are you sure?" My mom asked.

"Yes. No matter how this baby was conceived, it's still a part of me. The baby is innocent, and I won't hold it accountable for the sins of its father."

The room erupted in soft cheers as Keon leaned over, giving me a peck on the lips while rubbing my stomach. I gotta admit it felt weird. I guess that was something I would have to get used to.

"You not even a little disappointed?" I asked Keon.

"Why would I be? I love everything about you, and that baby is a part of you." He smiled.

"Congratulations, "Brielle said as she bent down to hug me, then squeezed between me and Jessica on the sofa. I nudged her with my elbow.

"So, cousin, how is the wedding planning going?" I asked.

"Girl, I stopped until you came home. The only thing I have is the venue." Brielle chuckled.

It warmed my heart to know that my cousin refused to continue her wedding plans without me but at the same time I hate that she put her life on hold for me. I hadn't realized I was crying until she wiped my tears and pulled me into an embrace. "I'm sorry"

"Don't apologize, it's not your fault. I'm just grateful to have you back. Now I can continue to plan." Brielle giggled, letting go of our embrace.

I smiled, "Really…"

CHAPTER 28

8 months later

The sun shone brightly over the garden, and the air was filled with excitement as guests arrived dressed in their finest attire, ready to witness the unity of souls in love. Soft music filled the air as guests took their seats on the rows of gold chairs that lined the outdoor courtyard. A hunter-green runner lay on the ground, six white columns were placed evenly along the border of the runner, leading the way to the altar.

A giant arch stood at the far end of the aisle. One column on each end of the arch was adorned with intricate floral arrangements in hunter green, gold, and white, featuring an abundance of roses, hydrangeas, and ferns, adding natural beauty to the scene. 'Best Part' by H.E.R. started playing, signaling the start of the ceremony.

Brielle stood on the balcony, watching the bridesmaids and groomsmen descend down the aisle to their assigned area. The women looked beautiful in their hunter-green dresses, and the handsome men wore white tuxedos and hunter-green vests.

"Please stand for the bride." The preacher announced at the change of the song.

'All of Me' by John Legend flowed through the speakers. "It's time," Brielle whispered with a nervous smile. Brielle picked up her bouquet and Ciera's and handed it to her.

"Oh my God, this is it." Ciera grinned.

Both girls separated and stood on the opposite end of the grand circular staircase. Brielle wore a white sweetheart lace wedding dress with a gold clasp in the center of her waist. The dress hugged every curve on her body. She wore her hair in a low bun with her flower leaf tiara that sparkled with rhinestones. Her veil was clipped just above her bun.

Ciera stood opposite Brielle wearing a sleeveless sweetheart gown, but instead of form-fitting, hers flowed freely, covering her protruding eight-month belly. She wore her curly hair in an updo, the tiara and veil adding to the beauty that radiated off her.

The song continued playing as Ciera and Brielle slowly descended the stairs, their trains dragging softly behind them. One handheld the bouquets and the other onto the stair rails.

Gerald held his hand out for Brielle as he watched from the bottom of the steps with tears, as this was the first time he had seen his daughter in her wedding dress. He not only cried happy tears but thankful tears that he was blessed with a second chance at life to walk his precious cupcake down the aisle.

Adjacent to Gerald stood Glen, who also held his hand out for Ciera as she neared the bottom of the staircase. All he could think about was how close he came to losing his one and only daughter. He thanked God for sparing her life and the baby growing inside her. Glen took comfort in the fact that Brayden was not Gerald's son. Although Glen despised who fathered the baby, it was still his grandchild none the less.

Once, Brielle and Ciera took their father's hand. They simultaneously looked into their daughter's eyes, taking in their beauty. They kissed their daughters on the cheek and intertwined their arms in theirs as they walked their daughters down the aisle. Loyal and Keon stood tall in their white tuxedos, their vision blurred by unshed tears as they watched their brides walk down the aisle towards them.

Brielle and Ciera reached the altar with gorgeous smiles as the grooms reached for their hand, releasing them from their fathers. Glen and Gerald turned around and sat beside their wives in the front row as the music faded.

"Dearly beloved, we gather here today to celebrate the union of Brielle and Loyal as well as Ciera and Keon in holy matrimony. Today, we witness the beautiful merging of four souls, four hearts, and four lives. Marriage is a sacred bond, a covenant between two individuals who have chosen to embark on a lifelong journey together. It is a commitment to love, honor, and cherish one another through all the joys and challenges that life may bring. If any of you show just cause why they should not be lawfully wed, speak now or forever hold your peace."

There was a moment of silence as the two couples gazed into each other's eyes.

"Well, alright!" The pastor smiled as he continued. "Who gives these two women to be married to these men?"

"I do." Glen and Gerald say together, standing up for their one-second spotlight and quickly sitting back down.

"As we stand here in the presence of God, let us remember the words of Apostle Paul: 'Love is patient, love is kind. It does not envy, it does not boast, it is not proud. It does not dishonor others, is not self-seeking, is not easily angered, and keeps no record of wrongs. Love does not delight in evil but rejoices with the truth. It always protects, always trusts, always hopes, always preserves.'

Brielle, Loyal, and Ciera, Keon, today you stand before each other and before God, ready to exchange your vows and commit to a lifetime of love and companionship. Your love is a testament to the power of connection and the beauty of finding your soulmate. Brielle, do you take Loyal and Ciera, do you take Keon to be your lawfully wedded husband, to have and to hold from this day forward, for better, for worse, in sickness and in health, for richer or poorer, forsaking all others, until death do you part?"

"I do," Both girls answer in unison.

"Loyal, do you take Brielle and Keon do you take Ciera to be your lawfully wedded wife, to have and to hold from this day forward, for better, for worse, in sickness and in health, for richer or poorer, forsaking all others, until death do you part?"

"I do," Both men answer in unison.

"As a symbol of your love and commitment, may we get the rings, please?"

The maid of honor, Jessica, and the best man, Trust, step forward, giving the pastor the rings. The pastor held the rings up, making sure not to mix them up.

"As you know, these rings are circular, with no beginning and no end, representing the eternal nature of true love. May they serve as a constant reminder of the vows you have made today."

The pastor held the rings out, and the couples grab the rings. "Grooms, place the ring on the left ring finger of your bride and repeat after me. I give you this ring as a symbol of my love, and with all that I am and all I have, I honor you, in the name of the Father, and of the Son, and the Holy Spirit." After the grooms completed their vows, the brides took their rings for them and repeated after the pastor placing rings on their fingers.

Now that Brielle, Loyal and Ciera and Keon have given themselves to each other by solemn vows, with the joining of hands and the giving and receiving of rings, I pronounce that they are husband and wife, in the name of the Father and the Son and the

Holy Spirit. Those whom God has joined together, let no one put asunder. Grooms, you may kiss your bride."

Brielle and Ciera both kiss their husbands, and the crowd erupts in cheer. Keon breaks away from Ciera to bend down and kiss her stomach before taking her back in his arms.

The preacher continues. "Ladies and gentlemen, it is with great pleasure that I present to you for the first time, Mr. and Mrs. Anderson," he points to Loyal and Brielle. "...and Mr. and Mrs. Wright." He points to Keon and Ciera. 'Marry You' by Bruno Mars booms through the speakers as the happy couples walk hand in hand down the aisle, eager to start their lives together as husband and wife.

The End

Epilogue

Brielle

"Happy birthday to you, happy birthday to you, happy birthday to Carson. Happy birthday to you!"

"Yay!" The crowd cheered as Ciera held Carson in her arms.

She kissed his chubby cheeks as he squirmed to get to his Baby Shark birthday cake. Ciera leaned over to help Carson blow out his candle, but not before he took a fist full of cake and stuffed it into his mouth, causing everyone to laugh.

Keon quickly passed the camcorder to Nathan as he ran over to take Carson from her. "I'll clean him up. Relax yourself, babe."

"Thanks," Ciera said as she sat down, out of breath. She rubbed her six-month belly as she smiled to herself, probably excited to meet her daughter in three months.

"How are you feeling?" I asked, sitting beside her.

"I'm good. I should be asking you that same question. You're pregnant with twins. How are you feeling?"

"I'm so ready for this to be over! I want my body back." I whined. "Everything is a struggle. I don't even know how my feet look anymore. Do my shoes match?"

Ciera laughed, "What shoes?" She asked, "You're barefooted."

"Dammit! That's another thing. I can't remember anything. Pregnancy brain is no joke." I laughed as I wiped a tear from my eye.

Ciera laughed. "Aint that the truth. You and Loyal pick out names yet?"

"Yeah. Justin and Journey." I answered proudly.

"I know Justice is happy." Ciera laughed. "Is that why she's going around, claiming him as her godson."

"Yep," I said, taking a deep breath.

We both got quiet as we watched the family dance in celebration of Carson's first birthday. Mike and Nova sat together, Mike feeding Nova as she fed their newborn daughter, Sage. The two ended up eloping after ten months of dating. Jessica and Trust danced together as she held Carson.

"Brielle, are you hungry?" Lisa yelled from the back sliding door. Before I could answer, I saw Loyal walking out with two plates. "I got it Mom." He says as he passes her, making his way towards me.

"What about you, Ciera?" Lisa asked.

"I'm good. Thanks, though." She answered.

"Nonsense. I'll make you a plate." She said before disappearing back inside the house.

"Thank you," I told Loyal as he sat my plate down. I quickly put a plastic plate over it that was left on the table to cover my food as he kissed me, then turned around and headed to the poker table with the rest of the men.

"You not hungry?" Ciera asked.

"No. I have heartburn." I say before letting out a long breath. I caught Ciera staring at Jessica and Trust as they danced with little Carson.

"I can't believe your brother-in-law and my sister-in-law are an item." She stated.

"I know, who would have thought?"

"No... Who would have thought about Mike and Nova." She chuckled.

"I know right!" I exclaimed. "Mike... the same guy who's been married to his job for years."

"The guy who claimed he never had time to date is married and has a baby. I never thought I would see the day. I'm happy for him." She stated.

I took another deep breath as I readjusted in my seat. I looked up as my mom, Aunt Sherry, and Lisa approached the table. Lisa handed a plate to Ciera. "Here you go, baby."

"Thanks Lisa," Ciera said.

The women took a seat around the table. "Brielle, I asked Justice and Honor to sort out the gifts. You have quite a few over there for the twins. Almost as many as Carson." My mom said.

"Thanks." I exhaled.

"Look at our men! All they do is play poker and talk crap." Aunt Sherry said.

"Girl, tell me about it. All Nathan would talk about is how he was about to take everyone's money." Lisa laughed. I took another deep breath.

"Keon is just as bad. I overheard him and Loyal talking about how Nathan's eyelid twitches when he's excited about a hand." Ciera said.

"Oh my god!" Lisa laughed. "So, how have you been Ciera?"

"I'm doing better, but I still have my moments. It's a night light in every room of my house, and I still can't walk to my car alone without getting paranoid."

"But you were doing so good with walking through parking lots," Aunt Sherry said, caressing Ciera's arm.

"I know... You know what? It might have gotten worse since I've been pregnant. Probably because I can't fully defend myself." Ciera said.

"That makes sense." My mom said. "I can't wait to meet your little girl Ciera."

I took another long exhale and shifted in my chair.

"I can't wait to meet my grandbabies either. Are you okay Brielle?" My mom asked, noticing my discomfort.

"Yeah, just a little heartburn."

"Heartburn? How long have you been feeling this." Aunt Sherry asked.

"Since yesterday, on and off throughout the day," I responded.

"Does your belly tighten up when it happens?" My mom asked.

"Yeah, a little," I said, getting up to go to the bathroom. Suddenly, a gush of wetness was felt between my legs. Did I just pee myself? I wondered.

"Honey, I don't think that's heartburn. I think you're in labor." My mom said.

"I think you may be right mom," I said, looking down at the ground. "My water just broke." A gasp can be heard around the table.

"Oh my God!" Aunt Sherry screamed, jumping up and down excitedly.

"Are you serious?" My mom gasped.

"You gotta go." All the women spoke at the same time.

"Loyal!" My mom and Aunt Sherry yelled at the same time. All the men looked back at us.

"My water broke!" I yelled.

"Showtime!" My dad grinned as all the men got up. "Ya'll head to the car. I'll lock up here and follow you guys to the hospital." I heard him say as Loyal rushed to me.

"Are you okay babe? Can you walk?" He asked, with worry in his voice.

Before I could give him an answer, I was hit with a wave of pain. I moaned and gripped my stomach as I notice the change in the intensity of the pain.

"Breath baby…" Loyal coached as I exhaled. My breathing calmed down. "Is it over?" he asked. I gave him a nod. "Alright, let's get to the car." He said as he guided me to the car. Followed by everyone else.

"Alright, I put the food inside," My mom yelled as she rushed out of the house. Let's go yawl... My grandbabies are coming!" She screamed.

Loyal gently helped me into the car and shut the door behind me. Swiftly, he made his way to the driver's side, anticipation evident in his hurried movements. As Loyal settled into the driver's seat, I secured my seatbelt. The engine roared to life, and we slowly pulled away from the familiar surroundings of my childhood home.

I watched in the rearview mirror the trail of vehicles that followed closely behind us. My family... my second chance to a life that held no regrets. Loyal grabbed my hand and kissed it. The weight of excitement and nervousness hung in the air, signaling the beginning of a new journey we were about to embark on.... Parenthood!

Made in the USA
Las Vegas, NV
24 January 2024

84867159R00138